What Do The Lonely Do At Christmas

KYIRIS ASHLEY

U.A.D PRESENTS

Stay Up to Date

To stay up to date on new releases, plus get information on contests, sneak peeks and more,

Click the link below...
https://mailchi.mp/6d21003686d1/subscribe

Soundtracks

Scan the QR Code below to listen to the Soundtracks/Singles of some of your favorite U.A.D titles:

Don't have Spotify or Apple Music?
No Sweat!
Visit your choice streaming platform and search URBAN AINT DEAD.

Currently on lock serving a bid?
JPay, iHeartRadio, WHATEVER!

We got you covered.
Simply log into your facility's kiosk or tablet, go to music and
search URBAN AINT DEAD.

URBAN AINT DEAD PRESENTS

Like & Follow us on social media:

FB - URBAN AINT DEAD

IG: @uadpresents

Tik Tok - @uadpresents

Submission Guidelines

Submit the first three chapters of your completed manuscript to
urbanaintdead@gmail.com, subject line: Your book's title. The
manuscript must be in a .doc file and sent as an attachment. The
document should be in Times New Roman, double-spaced, and
in size 12 font. Also, provide your synopsis and full contact
information. If sending multiple submissions, they must each be
in a separate email. Have a story but no way to submit it
electronically? You can still submit to URBAN AINT DEAD.
Send in the first three chapters, written or typed, of your
completed manuscript to:

URBAN AINT DEAD
P.O Box 448
Maybrook, NY 12543

DO NOT send original manuscript. Must be a duplicate.
Provide your synopsis and a cover letter containing your full
contact information.
Thanks for considering URBAN AINT DEAD.

Chapter One

The smell of Pine-Sol and apple cinnamon candles filled the air. Bianca had just finished cleaning her house and was now getting dressed to go to the grocery store to get the last few items she needed to prepare Christmas dinner. She'd opened all her curtains to let a little sunlight in, and the view of the freshly fallen snow from her windows was beautiful. After sliding a pair of dark washed jeans over her round, plump ass, she tugged a cream-colored turtleneck sweater over her head. She rubbed her hands over her perky C-cup breasts, smoothing the soft fabric over her skin.

At forty-two years old, Bianca didn't look a day over thirty. The phrase Black don't crack had to have been made especially for her. She took her bonnet off before taking the rollers out her hair. The full curls from the twenty-five inch lace front her stylist installed the day before framed her face, the jet black hair looking good against her caramel complexion. She placed a small pair of gold hoops in her ears before spraying on Valentino Donna Born In Roma Intense. She then slid her feet into a pair of wheat colored Timbs. She grabbed her caramel Louis Vuitton bag and put on her light brown leather jacket before opening her door.

It was just a few days before Christmas, and the cold December air hit her as soon as she walked out her house. Even in the cold Detroit air, nothing could take the smile off her face. Both her children were coming home for Christmas, and she couldn't wait to see them. Her twenty-two-year-old son, Lake, lived in New York, where he'd moved two years ago. Although they spoke often, he only came back home twice a year, once for Bianca's birthday and the other for Christmas. Her nineteen-year-old daughter, Journey, was away at college at Spelman in Atlanta. Although she came home more often than Lake, Bianca was excited for them to all be together.

She'd decorated her seven-foot Christmas tree in brown and gold a few weeks earlier and had begun wrapping all the gifts she'd bought with wrapping paper of the same colors. She'd been making a list of everything her children had told her they wanted or needed since October and had it all wrapped up under the tree waiting on them. She was making a huge Christmas dinner with all the trimmings, and she knew the stores would be packed this close to Christmas. So, she was prepared to spend a couple hours inside. She made her way to Kroger with soulful Christmas music playing through her speakers.

Just as she thought, Kroger's parking lot was packed. After about five minutes of driving around the parking lot, Bianca was finally able to find a parking spot. Next was the challenge of finding a shopping cart. After walking through the parking lot for a full two minutes, she finally came across an older woman pushing her empty cart back toward the door.

"Are you done with that?" Bianca asked with a smile, pointing down at the cart.

"Yes, I was just returning it. You can take it if you need it."

"Thank you! Happy holidays," Bianca replied, taking the cart and pushing it into the store.

Reaching into her purse, Bianca pulled out the folded piece of notebook paper that she'd written her shopping list on. She walked through the aisles, crossing things off her list, as she put them inside her cart. When she finally crossed the last item off her list, she made her way up to the checkout lines which were halfway through the aisles. After about twenty minutes of standing in line, she finally made it up to the register and paid for her items.

After leaving Kroger, Bianca decided to stop by Walmart and see if she could find her and her children matching pajamas. They used to wear them all the time back when the children were little, and Bianca thought that a bit of nostalgia would put a smile on all their faces. She found them all a pair of dark blue, satin pajamas with tiny Christmas trees printed all over them. Putting them into her cart, she continued walking through the store, heading over to the toy section. She picked up Uno Attack and Sorry, just in case they wanted to play a game on Christmas Eve the way they used to back in the day.

By the time Bianca made it back home, it was just after three in the afternoon. She put everything away before taking the turkey from the freezer and placing it into the sink to thaw out. After pouring herself a glass of wine, she prepared herself a salad and ate in her living room in front of the TV while watching *This Christmas*, her favorite Christmas movie. When the movie was done, she watched *Almost Christmas* before getting up to put fresh sheets and comforters on the beds in her children's old rooms.

By the time Bianca finished placing the last pillow on her daughter's bed, it was a little after eight at night. Boyz II Men's *Let It Snow* played through the house, and Bianca sang along, as she walked out the room, closing the door behind her. She stretched her back, feeling the long day in her muscles. Walking into the bathroom, she placed rollers into her hair before putting her bonnet on. She filled the tub, pouring bubble bath inside, as the steam carried the scent of eucalyptus through the air. She lit three candles, giving the bathroom a soft glow. Taking off her clothes, Bianca slid down into the hot water.

Bianca stayed in the tub until the water turned cold, and when she finally got out, she wrapped herself in her robe before blowing the candles out and walking back into her room. She'd just finished oiling her body when her phone rang. Looking down at the screen, she saw it was her best friend, Tasha.

Bianca smiled and answered. "What's up, my girl?"

"Nothing much, just callin' to check in on you. Did Lake and Journey fly in yet?"

"Not yet. Lake lands tomorrow morning around eleven, and Journey comes in at four in the afternoon. I can't wait to see them. I'm going to cook tomorrow when they get here. You should come over. I already know you gone be busy on Christmas Eve and Christmas day, so if you don't come tomorrow, then you probably gonna miss them this year."

"I thought they was already here, so I was gonna come over. But I'll be over tomorrow evening if it don't snow too bad. You know they saying we gone get twelve to fifteen inches starting tomorrow night," Tasha informed.

"Girl, this Michigan. They say we gon' get twelve to fifteen, but we probably gonna end up with four to six. It ain't gon' be no blizzard like they tryna say it's gon' be. You know them weathermen are the only people that can constantly do they job wrong and never get fired."

"Now you right about that. And in Michigan, it could be winter one day and summer the next. They sayin' we getting snow when really it could be sixty-five degrees and sunny. You remember that Christmas we had a few years back when it was damn near seventy degrees outside, then two days later, it was a foot of snow."

"Girl, or that winter that we had a snow storm and a thunderstorm at the same time. I ain't never seen no lightning with snow. I swear that's gotta be some shit that would only happen in Michigan," Bianca joked.

"What color decorations did you use this year? I already know you got that house looking like something out of a luxury magazine," Tasha spoke, changing the subject.

"Girl, the house is beautiful. I have it decorated in chocolate brown and gold. It's the first year that I've done these colors, and it looks so elegant. I got Journey's room all fixed up and even put up her small Christmas tree that was in her room every year when she was little. But it's pink and white like always. And I got Lake's favorite blanket at the foot of his bed and the mini fridge in his room filled with water and Gatorade like it always was. I got us all matching pajamas and everything. This will for sure be a Christmas to remember."

Tasha hummed knowingly. "I already know you miss them. You know you still got time to have another one. You don't have to be an empty nester just yet."

"Of course I miss them," Bianca whispered. "This house don't feel the same without them here everyday. But I don't know about having another one. I'm forty-two. I'm not sure I could even handle a baby at this age."

"Yeah, I hear you on that. I think you just used to being needed, and it's nothing wrong with that. You're just a good mama."

Bianca felt her throat tighten a little, and she swallowed it down. "Yeah... but it's more than that, Tash. I guess I just never thought about the time they would actually have to come home for the holidays. It's like I blinked, and they were grown."

"I get it. But you do know that's what happens, right? As the years go by, children age, and once they get grown, they move out. Well, unless you my brother, Robert, and you still living with our mama at thirty-eight years old. And I'm sure you don't want that. You did good, B. You raised two great children that turned into mature adults. You should be proud of yourself."

"I am proud of myself. That don't stop me from missing them though," Bianca replied, getting into bed and getting under the covers.

They continued to talk for about twenty more minutes before ending the call. Turning on her TV, Bianca opened the YouTube app and turned on ASMR before cutting off her lights. She allowed the TV to play, as she listened to the sounds until she fell asleep.

Chapter Two

Bianca woke up the next morning to the sun peeking in through her curtains. She rolled over, looking at the clock on her nightstand. It was a little after seven in the morning. Standing up from her bed, she stretched before making her way to the bathroom. She peed, washed her face, and brushed her teeth before heading down to her kitchen to make herself a smoothie. When she was done, she put on a pink, two-piece, workout set before heading down to her basement. Bianca had turned the room in the basement into a home gym, equipped with everything that she needed to keep her body tight.

If Bianca didn't do anything else, she was going to work out. She didn't play around about her fitness. That was how she looked so good at the age she was. She turned on her Bluetooth speaker and queued up her favorite workout playlist. It was a mix of 90's rap and R&B. Bianca climbed onto the treadmill, starting slow, before finding her rhythm.

Her feet hit the belt steadily, as her breath deepened. Sweat beaded down her temples, collarbone, and over the curve of her stomach as she ran. She pushed herself through the last ten minutes, the music pumping her up to go harder. When the treadmill beeped to signal the hour was up, she stepped off with shaky legs, breathing hard.

"That's enough," she muttered to herself, grabbing a bottled water from the small table in the corner of the room.

She walked upstairs, wiping her face with the towel she'd thrown across her neck. The house still smelled faintly like the candles she'd burned the night before. She headed straight to the bathroom, eager for a hot shower. Steam filled the room within seconds. Bianca stepped under the water, letting it wash away the sweat and tension from her workout. A smile spread across her face when she thought about the fact that in a few short hours, her children would be back home, and her family would be back together again. Her heart warmed just thinking about it.

After twenty minutes, she finally got out, wrapping a plush towel around her body. She was still wet when her phone rang. Looking down at her screen, she smiled when she saw it was her son, Lake.

"Hey, baby, you on your way to the airport? I can't wait to see you. I got..."

"Ma..." Lake interrupted, not allowing her to finish her statement.

Bianca's stomach dropped. "What's wrong?"

He exhaled. "My flight got canceled."

She froze. "Canceled? What you mean canceled?"

"The snowstorm, Ma. They canceling all the flights."

Bianca rushed over to the window, opening her curtain and looking out. "It ain't even that much snow on the ground. It's like two inches. That ain't nothing."

"It's bad down here, Ma. They said no flights are going out until at least the day after Christmas. Maybe longer."

Bianca sat on the edge of the tub, towel still wrapped around her. "But... it's Christmas. You're supposed to be here."

"I know," he spoke softly. "I'm still at the airport now. They trying to rebook everybody. But it ain't looking good. I'm probably not gonna make it home in time for Christmas, Ma."

Bianca didn't say anything for a second. Her chest tightened, as tears came to her eyes. Christmas without Lake wouldn't feel like Christmas at all.

"Are you okay? Do you need me to send you some money for a hotel? I don't want you driving in all that snow. How far away do you live from the airport?"

"I'm good, Ma. I'm only about fifteen minutes from the airport. I'ma go home and wait it out. I just wanted to let you know what was going on. I'm sorry, Ma. I know how much us being together for Christmas means to you."

Bianca's heart broke. "Don't be sorry, baby. It's not your fault. I just wanted you home, that's all. But what's most important is that you're safe."

"Yeah, I'm good, Ma. I'll text you when I get home and let you know I made it. As soon as the flights start going back out, I'm coming."

"Okay, baby. Be careful."

"I will."

"I love you, Lake."

"Love you too, Ma."

For a moment, she just sat there, staring at the floor, towel wrapped tightly around her like it was holding her together. Bianca closed her eyes, as the tears ran down her cheeks. She wanted her family together for the holiday, and now, her son wouldn't be able to come home. Disappointed was an understatement. She was plain old hurt. She was just full of joy, and now, her heart was heavy.

She walked into her room with her head down. She slipped into a pair of sweatpants and a shirt, not knowing what to do next. Her mood had changed, and the once jovial feeling was gone. Although her daughter was still coming, it wouldn't be the same without both of her children home. Bianca walked into the kitchen and stared at the counter filled with cooking supplies she planned to use on Christmas Eve. She'd told herself that she was going to cook her children a welcome home dinner tonight, but now with Lake not coming, she felt like ordering takeout for her and Journey would be better.

Opening her cabinet, she grabbed a mug and made herself a cup of peppermint tea. While the tea brewed, she leaned against the counter and stared out the window. *I knew we wasn't going to get the snow they said we would get,* she thought. Bianca took her tea into the living room and curled up on the couch, legs tucked under herself. She pulled the Christmas blanket Journey gifted her last year over her lap and stared at the tree and the gifts underneath that she'd wrapped in gold and chocolate brown wrapping paper, gifts that her son was now not going to open on Christmas morning. She felt the sting behind her eyes again.

"No," she whispered to herself. "I'm not crying no more today. Journey is still coming, and we gon' have fun."

She took a sip of tea and sat up straighter. Crying wouldn't change the weather. Crying wouldn't get her son home. She stood to her feet and began straightening her already spotless living room. She fluffed pillows that didn't need fluffing, adjusted stockings that were already perfectly even, and wiped down a coffee table that was spotless. She moved from room to room, sipping her tea and cleaning things that were already clean, just needing something to do with her hands.

When the tea was gone, she took her cup to the kitchen, washing it out before going into her home office. She'd told herself that she was going to take some time off work, but now with the way she was feeling, she knew she needed to do something to take her mind off the fact that her son was going to spend Christmas alone. As an author, Bianca was able to make her own schedule, and she knew nothing would take her mind off of the situation like writing a few thousand words of the book she was currently working on.

Sitting at her desk, Bianca powered on her laptop and opened the document. She wrote a few words, then her eyes drifted to the window. No matter how hard she tried, the words just wouldn't come out. After about twenty minutes of pretending to work, she shut the laptop and rubbed her temples. Standing up, Bianca slipped into her boots, threw on her thick coat, and stepped outside onto the porch. The cold hit her immediately. She crossed her arms and breathed out slowly, watching her breath fog the air. The street was quiet with no one outside, and

Bianca could only imagine the fun her neighbors were having with their families.

Bianca pulled her coat tighter around her, standing outside until her fingertips were numb. She took several deep breaths before walking back into the house. After hanging her coat back up, she sat on the couch and began flipping through Netflix. She settled on *Average Joe*, pressing play on the first episode, before looking over at the clock on the wall. It was a quarter to twelve, and she decided she would sit on the couch and watch TV until it was time to pick up Journey from the airport.

The second episode had just started when Bianca's phone rang. Looking down at her screen, her heart dropped when she saw Journey's picture flashing across it.

"Hello?" she answered quickly, hoping nothing was wrong.

"Mommy, they canceled my flight. They say it's a lot of snow up north, so no flights are going that way. Was Lake's flight canceled too, or is he there already?" Journey's voice spoke into the phone.

Bianca wanted to drop the phone, as tears came right back to her eyes. The realization that neither one of her children would be home for Christmas was hitting her hard.

"No, his flight was cancelled too," she spoke through her tears.

Her heart was breaking into piece inside her chest, and there was nothing she could do about it. All the plans she'd made, all the gifts she'd bought, and the decorating she'd done were all for nothing. Her Christmas was now ruined, and she would be spending it alone.

Chapter Three

Bianca cried for what seemed like hours. Even though she tried to hide it from her daughter, her feelings were crushed. It was the day before Christmas Eve, and neither one of her children would be home for the holidays. Her phone rang again, but Bianca couldn't take any more bad news, so she just let it ring. Walking to the kitchen, she poured herself a much-needed glass of wine before making her way back to her couch. When her phone rang again, Bianca thought it might be an emergency, so she picked it up. Looking at the screen, she saw it was Tasha and swiped the talk button.

"Hey, girl, what you over there doing? You started cookin' yet?"

"I'm not even cooking. The kids not coming. Both of their flights got canceled because of the snow."

"The snow? Ain't even no snow outside. They trippin'. This Michigan, a little snow ain't never hurt nobody."

"That's what I said. But from what Lake said, it's snowing bad in New York, and Journey said that a lot of states up north got a lot of snow. So, that's stopping the flights. I'm so sad because I was ready for them to be here. I had everything all planned out, so we would have a great time. And now, we not even gonna be together." Bianca began to cry.

"Aw, B, don't cry. Everything is going to be fine. You can always come to my house for Christmas. And tonight, I'm going to this party in West Bloomfield. Nah, fuck that. We going to this party in West Bloomfield ."

"A party? I don't even feel like going nowhere, let alone a party."

"And that's exactly why you going. Now get sexy and I'll be there at nine to pick you up. I don't want to hear no bullshit because I'm not taking no for an answer."

Tasha gave no time for Bianca to say no, ending the call as soon as she finished her sentence. Bianca didn't want to go anywhere. What she wanted was to spend the holidays with her children. And if she couldn't do that, then she would much rather spend her time lying in bed. However, she knew if Tasha said she would be there at nine, then she was going to be there. So, with that, Bianca got up and walked to her closet, trying to find something to wear. After about forty-five minutes of looking and not finding anything she liked, she finally decided on a long sleeved, black, bodycon dress. She chose to pair it with a pair of knee-high black boots and her black Chanel bag.

Bianca took her time curling her hair, not because she wanted it to look perfect for the night but because she didn't actually want to go. When she was done, she put on her makeup before finally getting dressed. She'd just sprayed herself with Dolce & Gabbana's Devotion when her doorbell rang. She already knew it was Tasha, but she looked out the peephole anyway before she opened the door.

"What up doe, bestie? You looking good," Tasha greeted, walking in and giving Bianca a hug.

Tasha stood about five feet three inches tall with flawless chocolate brown skin that somehow always glowed. Her brown hair was in long, flowing curls down her back with lighter brown streaks through them. She wore a short, black, leather skirt with black fishnet stockings underneath. She also wore a black bustier with a black leather jacket over it. They had been friends for years, and while Bianca seemed to always be the put together friend, Tasha was the rebel.

"Thank you. You look good too. And where are we going again?"

"To this Christmas party downtown. The flyers been all over Instagram. I know you seen them. This 'bout to be the party of the year."

Bianca rolled her eyes. "I would just much rather stay home in my bed with a glass of wine and a good Christmas movie. I just don't feel like being around people right now."

"Right, so you can cry yo' lonely ass to sleep? Girl, definitely not. We going out, and we gon't have a good time. Now, grab your coat so we can go."

"Fine, but I feel like I should drive my own car so that I can leave when I'm ready. I already know you gon' try to stay until the lights come on. I want to leave way before that."

"And that's exactly why you not driving yoself. Stop acting like some old, wrinkled ass lady. You gon' shake that ass tonight and like it. Now come on!"

With that, Bianca slid her coat on and followed Tasha out to her Jeep. Bianca sat in the car, looking out the window the entire time. Tasha, on the other hand, was the total opposite, snapping her fingers and singing along to every song she played on the way there. Every now and then, she would tap Bianca's thigh or nudge her shoulder, trying to lighten her mood. Bianca would give a half smile each time she looked over at her.

"You might as well fix your face right now because we having fun tonight. I know you sad, friend, and that's all the more reason why you need to have a good time tonight. I know you wanted to spend the holidays with the kids, but the flights got canceled. But the good news is they're safe. And they are still coming. It's not today, but you will still see them. The presents will still be there, along with everything else you bought. So, you can still have Christmas together. It just may not be on Christmas day."

Bianca nodded, knowing that what Tasha was saying was true.

Her children being safe was the most important thing. And just because they didn't spend time together on Christmas day didn't make the time they would spend together any less special. Bianca took a deep breath, trying to calm the sadness she felt in her heart. She wanted to say something but was afraid she would burst out into tears, so instead, she just nodded her head.

Tasha looked over at Bianca. "Oh, hell no! Stop that sad shit now." She turned up the volume when Cardi B's *WAP* came on and sang along. "You need to be trying to find you somebody tonight, so you can start giving that wet ass pussy away. That shit probably ain't been used since Obama was president."

"Please shut up. I've had sex since then," Bianca uttered, looking at Tasha from the corner of her eye.

"Have you had sex this year? Or even last year? Better yet, what year was it the last time you had sex? I'll wait." Tasha laughed at her own joke, as she waited for Bianca to answer.

"How 'bout you worry about your own pussy? I highly doubt I'll meet anyone at this party tonight that I would want to give my pussy to."

"Girl, please. Ain't nobody worried about yo' pussy. I'm worried about you not getting no dick. I just don't want you to turn into one of them miserable old ladies that be yelling at kids to stay off they lawn."

"Girl, please. I ain't miserable. I just miss my kids, and I'm sad I'm not going to be with them for Christmas. That's it."

"Okay, you got it, sis. I just don't want you to be sad. That's all."

About fifteen minutes later, the mansion came into view. Bianca's eyes widened, as she looked at the huge house. Tasha turned onto the long driveway and pulled up to the guarded gate.

"Name?" the tall, muscular, clearly armed guard asked.

"Tasha McCall and this is my plus one," Tasha informed, pointing over at Bianca.

The guard looked over the list, nodding when he found Tasha's name. "I see you. We have to keep a record of everyone that attended the party tonight. So, I'm going to need your friend's name as well."

"Bianca Thomas," Tasha replied.

The man nodded, writing Bianca's name on the list, before opening the gate and allowing them inside.

"Girl, whose party did you say this was? This is a nice ass house."

"This guy named Maceio. He a big fish in the city as you can see. He has a huge ass Christmas party every year, but this is the first time I was able to get on the list."

"Damn..." Bianca breathed. "I wonder what kind of money you gotta make to live in a house like this?"

"Bitch, a lot."

The venue was an old historic estate on the river, and it was lit from top to bottom. Spotlights washed the front in soft gold, and two huge nutcrackers flanked the double doors. The circular driveway was filled with luxury cars, and Bianca couldn't help but to think that the entire city had come out to party with whoever Maceio was. Valet workers jogged through the cold, rushing to open doors for guests dressed to the nines. Music played from inside, but it wasn't Christmas music. It was a mix of hip hop and R&B.

Tasha pulled up to the front, and one of the valets jogged over with a smile on his face. "Evening, ladies," he spoke, as he opened Tasha's door for her to step out.

Bianca stepped out the passenger's side, the cold air nipping at her before she pulled her long, black coat tighter around her. She watched as Tasha handed the valet her keys, and she walked around the car toward Bianca.

"You ready?" Tasha asked, looking over at Bianca

Bianca exhaled. "Let's do it."

They walked up the steps, heels clicking against the salted concrete. Before they reached the door, Bianca stopped, looking up at the house once more.

"You good?" Tasha asked.

"Yeah, I'm good. I'm just taking it all in, that's all. But let's go. I'm ready to see the rest of the house."

They stepped through the double doors and made their way into the party. Inside, the house was transformed into a winter wonderland. A massive Christmas tree stood in the center of the foyer, decorated with gold and white oversized ornaments, twinkling lights, and a star that sparkled like real crystal. Garlands draped the grand staircase, and a DJ booth was set up in the corner blasting music. As they walked farther into the home, they saw an open bar in one room stocked with nothing but top shelf liquor and champagne. Across from that were several long tables filled with several different entrees. Everything from lobster tails to fried chicken sat along the table.

The house was packed with what seemed to be hundreds of people, but the huge house wasn't overcrowded. Even with all the bodies that filled it, Bianca was still able to move around comfortably.

"Come on, B. Let's go get us a little something to eat before we start drinking," Tasha suggested.

"Girl, you drove. Yo' ass won't be drinkin' much of nothing."

"Girl, please. You think I'ma waste a night like this being sober? Look around you, we gon' have a good time tonight. Worst case, we take an Uber home, and I get my car in the morning."

"I'll just not drink before we have to do all that."

Tasha rolled her eyes. 'Bitch, any excuse for you not to have some fun. Girl, loosen up. Now, come on so we can get some of that lobster before it's all gone."

Bianca nodded, knowing this was a battle that she wouldn't win, and walked over to the buffet with Tasha. They both placed a few items on a small plate, Tasha singing along to Nicki Minaj as she drizzled butter onto her lobster. Bianca took a seat at one of the tables on the far side of the room, as she waited on Tasha to join her.

"Girl, why is that fine ass man over there checking you out?" Tasha whispered, as she took her seat.

"Girl, what? Please stop. Ain't nobody checking me out. And even if they were, I'm good. I'm not looking for no man."

"You might not be looking for one, but one might have found you. And he's walking over here right now."

Bianca looked up from her plate in time to see a man holding a small glass of brown liquor in his hand. He was tall, six five, with a muscular build. The waves in his jet-black hair were deep, and his thick beard was neatly lined. He wore a black Gucci sweater and a pair of black Gucci pants. His dark chocolate skin was flawless, and his watch and chain he wore showed Bianca that he made a lot of money.

"Good evening, ladies. I hope the two of you are enjoying the party," he spoke, looking between them both before fully turning his attention to Bianca. "I couldn't help but notice how beautiful you look tonight, and I had to come introduce myself. My name is Wise." He smiled, showing all thirty-two of his beautifully white teeth.

"Hello, Wise. My name is Bianca, and this is my friend, Tasha. We just got here, but the house is beautiful, and I'm sure the party will be great as well."

"Yeah, these parties always be lit. It's the one night where you can find all the high rollers in the city in one place without no bullshit going on."

"Do you come to these parties every year?" Tasha asked, looking up at Wise.

"I have for the last three years. However, this is the first time I've seen the two of you here.'

"This is both of our first time," Bianca replied with a smile, as she looked up into Wise's deep brown eyes.

"Oop, there go Keisha and nem. I'll be right back," Tasha chimed in, already sliding her chair back before Bianca could protest.

"Tasha..." Bianca started, but it was too late. Her friend tossed her a mischievous smirk over her shoulder and disappeared into the crowd.

Bianca slowly turned back, not believing that Tasha had just left her sitting there with a stranger. The man was fine, Bianca had to admit that, but the fact still remained that she didn't know him.

"Damn, she got up quick. That must mean that she wants us to talk." He smiled.

Bianca smiled back but didn't reply, mainly because she didn't know how to. It had been years since she'd even so much as been on a date with a man. And now here one was, standing there and clearly flirting, and Bianca had no clue what to do. For a moment, they didn't speak, just looked at each other. However, the moment was awkward but rather peaceful.

Wise's voice was smooth when he finally spoke again. "I've been tryin' to figure out where I know you from."

"You don't," Bianca replied gently, keeping her eyes locked on him.

"Nah, I might. One thing I'm not going to forget is a face. Especially one as beautiful as yours."

She smiled. "Well, I'm from the city, so maybe that's where you know me from."

"Maybe, but I've seen you before. That part I'm sure of."

"You here with yo' girl? Because you don't look like the type that will come out to a party alone."

Wise chuckled. "You got me pegged already?"

"Maybe. But am I right is the real question."

"Well, you're kind of right. I didn't come here by myself. But I'm not with my woman because I don't have one of those. I came with my brother and my cousin. They around here somewhere. What about your man?"

Her breath caught. *My man?* she thought. *I haven't had a man since I broke up with the last guy I was dating over five years ago. The fact that he thought I had one must mean I still got it.*

"I'm single," Bianca replied.

She wasn't looking for a man at all. However, Tasha had all but dragged her to this party and now had disappeared. So, if this handsome man wanted to keep her company while she was there, then she would let him.

"Would you like a drink?"

"No, thank you. I know my friend is going to be drinking tonight, so I'm almost certain I'll have to drive us home."

"Got you. Well, do you mind if I take a seat?" he asked, nodding down at the chair Tasha had abandoned.

"Sure, go head."

Wise smiled, taking his seat. "So, you still not going to tell me where I know you from? Because I'm telling you I've seen you before."

Bianca smiled. "Do you read?" she asked, wiping her hands with a napkin before tossing it on her half empty plate.

Wise frowned. "What type of question is that?"

"I'm asking because I write books. And if you do a lot of reading, then you probably have seen my face on the back of one of my books."

"You write books?" Wise pulled out his phone. "What's your last name?"

"Thomas, but I write under the name Bianca T."

Bianca watched as he put her name into his Google search. His mouth dropped open when all the books she'd written popped up. She didn't take him as a person that would have read anything she'd written. However, when he continued telling her that he knew her, she thought that maybe he'd actually read one.

"Yo! You famous as hell, my baby. My sister got all these shits. I knew I knew you from somewhere. This is so dope. How long have you been writing?"

"Thank you. And I've been writing all my life. But I didn't publish my first book until ten years ago. Writing has always been my passion, and I was able to turn my passion into a career."

"Damn, ten years? You must have started publishing young as hell. How old were you when you published your first book?"

Bianca smiled at Wise. She was used to people questioning her age, thinking she was younger than what she actually was. It didn't bother her at all. At forty-two years old, Bianca liked walking into the store and getting carded for a bottle of wine.

"I started publishing at thirty-two," Bianca spoke then sat back in her seat, as she waited on the reply she knew was coming.

"Thirty-two? You were thirty-two ten years ago? It's no way you in your forties right now."

Bianca smiled. "I can assure you that I am. I know I have a baby face, and most people think I'm in my twenties. I'm sure that's what you thought when you approached me. So, now I have to ask how old you are."

"I'm thirty," he replied.

Chapter Four

Bianca sat across from Wise, listening to him talk, however all she could hear was him telling her he was thirty years old, twelve years her junior. She knew he was a bit younger than her, but she thought he was at least thirty-five. *Seven years wouldn't be so bad but twelve? I ain't got time to be fuckin' with no young actin' nigga,* she thought. She looked at his face, his smooth flawless skin, and his neatly trimmed, full beard.

Bianca blinked at him, sure she'd heard wrong. "Wait... did you say *thirty*?"

Wise nodded, downing the last of his drink. "Yeah. My birthday is in July."

Her instinctive reaction must've shown on her face because Wise chuckled, leaning back just enough to give her space. "That a problem?"

"I wouldn't say a *problem*." Bianca smoothed her hand across her thigh. "Just surprising, that's all."

"Mm." Wise shrugged, unbothered. "People always think I'm older."

"You look older," she admitted. "Not in a bad way. I guess you just give grown man energy."

"And you now look like you're tryin' to figure out if you should keep talkin' to me or not."

Bianca laughed despite herself. "Maybe a little."

"Well," he spoke, eyes meeting hers, "we just talkin', right?"

"Exactly," Bianca agreed, feeling her shoulders relax. "Just talking."

"Cool. So, let's talk," Wise replied with a sly smile.

With that, they continued their conversation. He told her he was born and raised on the Eastside and started out working in construction with his uncle before starting his own company. He told her that he liked old-school R&B more than rap despite looking like he'd be the opposite. She told him a little about her children, the holiday traditions they still tried to keep, and how neither of them were able to come home this Christmas.

Her mood was now lighter, and she was enjoying her conversation with Wise and decided that maybe she would have a drink.

"You know what?" she uttered. "I think I'm going to have a drink with you. Only one though."

"Then let's get it."

He guided her toward the bar, not touching her but walking close enough that she felt his energy with every step. The bar glowed in warm reds and golds, the bartender sliding glasses across polished wood. Bianca rested her elbow on the counter and ordered. "French 75 please."

Wise smirked. "Ohhh, we fancy, huh?"

Bianca laughed. "And what's your drink?"

"Hennessy on the rocks." Wise spoke to the bartender while looking at Bianca.

"Of course it is."

He grinned. "What is that supposed to mean? Hennessy is a classic."

Their drinks came quickly. Bianca lifted hers, the glass cool against her fingers, and took a slow sip. "Mmm," she murmured. "That's good."

They stood shoulder to shoulder, talking over the music yet still hearing each other clearly. The liquor warmed her chest, loosening the rest of her nerves. Then his hand lightly brushed the bar near hers, not touching, just close.

"You wanna dance?"

Bianca hesitated only a second. She was feeling good, and the vibe was right. And she couldn't deny the way Wise was looking at her.

"Yes," she agreed.

"Great, come on then."

They walked to the dance floor where the crowd swayed under soft lights and holiday décor. An old school jam by Blackstreet drifted through the speakers. Wise placed his hands respectfully on her waist, not grabbing, just guiding. Bianca slipped her arms around his shoulders, surprised at how natural it felt. It was almost as if they had done this before. One song turned into two then three. By the fourth, Bianca's cheeks were warm, and her body felt lighter than it had in days.

"You alright?" he asked softly.

"Yeah," she breathed. "I'm good."

Another song started, but Bianca's mouth was dry now, and she needed something to slow the pace of whatever was building between them. She gently stepped back, smoothing her dress.

"I think I need another drink."

Wise raised an eyebrow. "Thought it was a one drink night for you?"

"It was," she replied, laughing, "but I changed my mind."

He smiled, and when he gently took her hand and led her to the bar, Bianca welcomed it, smiling, as she followed him. They ordered their second round of drinks and chatted close to the bar as they sipped. Bianca found Wise intriguing and was now glad that he'd stopped to talk to her. She hadn't even wanted to come out tonight but was now having a great time, and she knew it was all because of him.

Hours felt like minutes as they passed. They danced and chatted more until Tasha finally made her way back over to them. Bianca could tell that she was a little tipsy as soon as she walked over.

"There you are and still with him. I been looking for you for the past thirty minutes, and you not even answering your phone.

I'm coming to give you my keys, so you can drive yourself home. I'll just come get my car in the morning," Tasha informed, handing Bianca her key fob.

"What? How the hell you just gon' leave me here when I came out with you? And where the hell you going?"

"I'm not leaving you, girl. If you want to leave right now, you can walk out with me. You just gotta drive yourself home because I'm going with Marty. It looks to me that you are already occupied and not ready to leave. So, stay with your newfound friend." Tasha took a step closer, leaning in and whispering so that only Bianca could hear her. "Maybe Mr. Sexy Face can knock the cobwebs off that pussy for ya."

Bianca just shook her head, hoping that Tasha had whispered that last part low enough for Wise not to hear her. She placed the key fob into her purse and told Tasha to text her when she got to where she was going. She watched as Tasha walked off with a tall, brown skinned man before turning her attention back to Wise. They continued to talk and sip, making enjoyable conversation. Bianca was surprised at how comfortable she felt with him and how easygoing he was.

Wise tilted his head toward her after a moment. "So, tell me, what made you decide to step out tonight? You don't strike me as a party-every-weekend type."

"I'm really not," Bianca admitted. "But my friend said that I needed to get out instead of sitting in the house sad about my kids not being able to fly home for Christmas. So, I came out with her, and this bitch left me." Bianca chuckled.

"She did, but she left you in good hands."

Smiling, Bianca took another sip, letting the champagne fizz against her tongue. "So, you said you come here every year. Is the party always this extravagant?"

"Absolutely, Maceio don't play no games when it comes to his Christmas parties."

The DJ switched the vibe, easing into a slower mix, as En Vogue came through the speakers. She watched as his gaze followed her body.

"You tryna dance again?" he asked.

Bianca hesitated just long enough for him to notice.

"I won't bite," he teased. "Not unless you ask me to."

Her breath caught. This time, when she placed her hand in his, they intertwined their fingers. They slipped into the crowd again, but it felt like the room shrank around them. Wise rested one hand at the small of her back, the other gently holding her waist. Bianca's arms slid over his shoulders, her fingers relaxing against the back of his neck. His body was warm and solid. They moved slow, swaying to a rhythm that had nothing to do with the song playing through the speakers. Bianca's heartbeat thudded softly in her chest, as Wise's fingertips gently brushed the small of her back.

Her entire body tingled when he pulled her closer, closing the small gap between them. They swayed through another song. For a moment, her mind drifted to her empty house with warm Christmas lights and presents that wouldn't be opened on Christmas morning. She exhaled slowly.

Wise must of felt it because he pulled back a little, looking down at her. "You okay? You looking like you have something on your mind all of a sudden."

"I'm sorry. I just thought about going back home later and how quiet it's going to be."

"You don't like quiet?" he asked, still looking down at her.

"I mean, I'm used to the house being quiet with me being the only person there. But I expected to spend the holiday with my kids. So, now, I'm going home to a house full of plans that's not going to happen."

"So, you don't want to be alone tonight?"

"No," she answered quickly – almost too quick.

Wise let his fingers lightly graze her waist, pulling her back into him.

"Do you live close by?" he asked, whispering into her ear.

"Not really, probably about thirty minutes."

A long beat passed before Wise replied again. "If company is what you want, then I can offer mine."

Bianca inhaled. Her nerves fluttered but not in fear, rather in anticipation. She hadn't had a man in her home who wasn't there to fix something in years. And maybe Tasha was right. She did need Wise to knock the cobwebs off her pussy.

"I wouldn't mind it," she replied.

Wise searched her face. "You sure?"

"Yes." She nodded. "I'm sure."

He nodded. "Then I'll ride with you."

Bianca's pulse thudded in her chest. She nodded her head, letting Wise know that she was ready when he was. Wise shot a quick text to his homeboys, letting them know that he was leaving. Bianca smiled as she watched him. When he took her hand this time, he led her to the door and outside. They walked over to the valet and told him which car was hers before it was in front of them moments later. The two of them got in with Bianca in the driver's seat, as they made their way to her house.

<h1 style="text-align:center">Chapter Five</h1>

When they arrived at Bianca's house exactly thirty minutes later, they got out, and Bianca led him inside. Walking him farther into the house, she showed him to the living room, letting him know that he could have a seat, before offering him something to drink. He opted for a bottle of water, and she returned with two. Taking her seat next to him on the couch, she opened the bottle and took a sip, as they sat in an awkward silence.

"Your decorations are beautiful," Wise spoke, finally breaking the silence.

"I'm sorry. I don't really do this," Bianca replied.

"Do what?"

"This. Bring men I just met to my home. Shit, or even meeting men for that matter. All this shit is new to me."

"It's okay, Bianca. I can promise you that we won't do anything that you don't want to do."

She smiled, nodding her head at his reassurance. She took a couple more sips of her water, still nervous, before asking if Wise would like anything stronger to drink. She told him that she didn't have Hennessy but did have a bottle of D'Ussé in the kitchen. Wise agreed, and within moments, Bianca was back and pouring the brown liquid into two glasses.

"Would you like me to put on some music or a movie or something? Or maybe we can just talk? I'm sorry. I know I'm bad at this."

"I wouldn't mind listening to some music," he replied.

Bianca nodded, picking up the remote from the coffee table and turning on Apple Music. *Sumthin' Sumthin'* by Maxwell filled the room as Wise smiled.

"Ah, naw, this my shit right here," Wise spoke, taking a drink from his glass.

Wise leaned back, stretching out a little, making himself more comfortable. Bianca took a sip from her glass then another. The warmth slid down her throat, loosening the tension in her shoulders. The song switched, and *Ascension* came on. Bianca loved this song, and she moved a little to the beat, as she sang along.

"Oh, I see you got good taste in music," Wise complimented, tapping his glass gently against hers, as they both downed the last of their drinks.

"Thank you. You said you like R&B more than rap and so do I. So, I figured I'd put on my go to playlist. Would you like another drink?"

Wise nodded, and Bianca poured them both another drink, as the song changed again, *Soulful Moaning* by Shawn Harris. By this time, Bianca had loosened up and was now standing and moving her hips slowly to the beat with the glass still in her hand. Wise smiled, downing his drink, before standing to his feet and joining her. He grinded slowly, as he made his way slowly to her, placing his hands on her hips. He guided her movements, as they grinded together, the music leading their rhythm. By the time Raphael Saadiq's *Ask of You* played, they had turned her living room into their own personal dance floor.

Wise's hands roamed her body, first the small of her back, then down her hips. And by the time After 7's *Ready or Not* played, Wise's hands were cupping her plump ass. She didn't stop him. In fact, she welcomed his touch, as she danced. Bianca wrapped her arms around his shoulders, as they swayed together. Busta Rhymes and Janet Jackson's *What's It Gonna Be* came on, switching the tempo a bit, and before Bianca knew it, their lips were pressed together in a slow, wet rhythm that took her breath away. His lips were soft, and the deeper the kiss got, the weaker her knees became.

Wise gripped her ass tighter, holding Bianca up without even knowing. She slowly ran her medium length, manicured nails over the back of his neck, as his tongue massaged hers. The gentle pressure of his mouth made her entire body unravel. She hadn't been kissed like that in a long time, but this didn't feel like a regular kiss. This was him sending heat through her veins that reminded her she was still a woman. This kiss let her know that she was still desirable, and even if it was just for one night, this man wanted her.

Wise pulled back just a little, breaking the kiss. He raised his hand, bushing his thumb against her cheek, his gaze locked on hers.

"Your lips taste good," he murmured.

Bianca smiled, her eyes locked on his.

"Now, I want to see if your other set of lips taste as sweet as these. Would you like that?"

Bianca looked up at him, shocked at first, but it only lasted for a second before she felt wetness pooling into her panties. She hadn't been touched like that in so long that she didn't even know if she still had what it took to please a man. But she knew she wanted it. She couldn't talk; her breath was caught. However, she was able to nod her head, and she did so slowly. Wise wasted no time, pulling her dress up over her hips before scooping her up into his arms. She wrapped her legs around his waist, leaning in to kiss him again. He walked over to the couch, never taking his lips off hers.

Wise laid Bianca down on the couch, and she looked up at him, as he removed his sweater. Bianca watched as he slid his shirt off, revealing the black beater underneath. His arms were muscular and covered with ink. Bianca bit her bottom lip in anticipation, her eyes locked on Wise. He leaned down on the couch and began pulling up her dress. Bianca lifted off the couch a bit so that he could pull it up farther then finally over her head. She laid back down, watching him admire her body that was now dressed in only black lace.

Slowly, Wise allowed his fingertips to travel down her stomach and over the curve of her hips. He leaned down, licking her naval, before pulling her panties down and tossing them onto the floor. Bianca spread her legs, flipping one over the couch, giving Wise a clear view of her glistening pussy. Bianca may not have had sex on the regular; however, she made sure to keep a fresh wax on her pussy. Wise leaned down again, this time positioning himself between her legs. He gripped her thighs, pulling her down and into his mouth. Bianca gasped when his wet tongue licked slowly over her love box, tasting her juices, before gently kissing her clit.

She hissed when he gently sucked then licked then sucked again. Before she knew it, her hand had traveled down to his head, wrapping around the back and pushing him in deeper. His mouth was wet, and his tongue was firm, and although Bianca hadn't been touched in a while, this had to be some of the best head she'd gotten in all her forty-two years of living.

"Fuckkkkkkkk," she breathed when Wise slid his tongue inside her. She wrapped one leg around his neck, holding him there, as she gripped both of her breasts.

"Damn, this shit taste better than the top lips," Wise mumbled in between licks. "This shit sweet as fuck."

Bianca couldn't control herself. Her entire body began to shake, as his tongue twirled slow circles around her love button. Her moans grew louder, as her climax neared. When she came, Wise cleaned up every drop. However, he didn't stop there. He continued to lick and suck until Bianca was begging for him to turn her loose. She sat up from the couch, chest heaving, as she looked over at him.

"Damn, you good at that."

"I hope you not tapping out because I'm just getting started."

Bianca bit her bottom lip. Her legs felt like Jello, as she tried to stand up. Pouring herself another drink, she took a sip before looking over at him. "I'm down to do whatever you want to do."

"Then let's go to your bedroom," Wise suggested.

Bianca nodded, taking her glass and the bottle of liquor and motioning for Wise to follow her. She led him through the house and up the stairs to her bedroom. Walking inside, she poured more liquor into both their glasses before lighting a few candles and turning out the lights, wanting to set the mood before they continued anything. When she was done, she took a sip of her drink before setting it on the nightstand.

Slowly, she walked over to Wise, standing between his legs. His hands rose up her thighs and ass. He tried to stand up, but Bianca stopped him, dropping to her knees in front of him. Their attraction was undeniable, and even though they'd just met, it felt like the heat had been building between them for years. She unbuckled his belt before unzipping his pants. He stopped her, standing to his feet to undress himself before sitting back on the bad. Bianca's eyes widened when she saw the length of his dick. Not only was it long, about ten inches if Bianca had to guess, but it was also thick with a small curve to it.

Bianca positioned herself back between his legs. Her mouth salivated from the sight. She took him into her hand, holding his manhood steady, as she allowed her saliva to run out of her mouth and drip onto the head of his dick. She then swirled her tongue over the head, causing Wise to make a low hissing sound. Once she was sure she'd done enough teasing, she took as much of him into her mouth as she could, using her hand to massage the length of his manhood that was left over. She watched as his hands gripped her comforter, and she knew she still had it. It had been a long time since Bianca had sucked a dick, but apparently, it was like riding a bike. Once you learned, you never forgot how to do it.

"Fuckkkkkk, my baby, let me find out that's how you give it up."

Bianca smiled inside, picking up her speed and tightening her jaws at the same time. Sweet precum slid from the head of his shaft and onto her tongue, and that only made her want to suck more. It was like getting to the cream filling of her favorite cake.

To Bianca, the cream was always the best part. She sucked and made loud slurping noises as she moaned. Bianca didn't know if it was the man or the liquor, but sucking his dick was getting her off just as much as him eating her pussy had.

Gently, Wise placed his hand on the back of her head, pushing his dick farther into her mouth. Bianca allowed it, letting his manhood travel deeper down her throat. With his other hand, he pulled one of her perky breasts from the cup of her bra and gently twirled her nipple between his thumb and index finger. Bianca moaned as she felt the tingle throughout her entire body.

"That's right, baby. You suckin' that dick. You gon' suck all that cum up out that muthafucka?"

"Mmhm," Bianca replied, mouth full of dick.

She continued to suck and slurp, occasionally looking up at him to see his head thrown back and him biting the hell out of his bottom lip. The sight of it was sexy to Bianca, and her juices pooled between her thighs. Before she knew it, Wise was moaning even louder, and hot cum was shooting down her throat. She swallowed all of it, licking it clean.

"Damn, my baby, that's what you on? Shitttt, tell a nigga you a freak without saying you a freak."

Wise stood to his feet, picking up his pants from the floor, before pulling out two condoms. He tossed one on the bed before opening the other and sliding it onto his dick and throwing the gold wrapper onto the floor. Bianca laid on her back with her legs spread wide. However, Wise grabbed one of her ankles and flipped her over on her stomach.

"Get on your knees," he ordered.

Bianca obliged, getting onto her hands and knees and arching her back. Wise got on his knees, sliding his tongue over her slit. She moaned loudly, feeling his wet tongue trail from her pussy to her asshole. Her eyes rolled in the back of her head, as his tongue flicked around her ass, making her pussy even wetter. It was like a river flowing between her legs, and Bianca had never been this wet before. When he stood up and lined his manhood up with her wetness and pushed in, Bianca let out a loud gasp, moaning at every inch that entered her, as Wise went deeper inside her.

"Damn, and this shit tight too. Fuck! A nigga done hit the jackpot."

Wise grabbed her lips, finding his rhythm, as Bianca matched it. The sound of moans and skin slapping filled the room. Wise was so deep inside her that Bianca swore she felt him in her stomach. Trailing his fingers up her back, Wise unhooked her bra before slowly running the straps over her shoulders with his hands and down her arms, stopping at her wrists. His touch alone sent chills down Bianca's body. She pulled her hands from the straps, tossing the bra on the floor, before Wise placed his hand around her neck, not choking, just holding. Then, he pushed her upward until they were back to chest.

"This pussy feel so good," he moaned into her ear.

Bianca bit her bottom lip, tossing her head back and laying it on Wise's shoulder. She wanted to tell him how good his dick felt, but she couldn't talk. Every time she opened her mouth to say it, moans were the only thing that left her lips. Letting go of her neck, Wise pushed her back down onto the bed, burying her face into the mattress, as he drilled her from behind. He slapped her ass, watching it jiggle, before grabbing her hips and drilling harder.

He pulled out, flipped her over on her back, and climbed on top of her. Bianca wrapped her legs around him, as he slid back into her, filling her up once more. This time, his rhythm was slower and deeper. When she clenched the walls of her pussy around his manhood, Wise damn near lost it.

"Oh, so you want this to be my pussy, huh? Keep doing shit like that and it's gon' be. You takin' all this dick too."

Putting his hands under her thighs and grabbing her wrists, Wise lifted Bianca off the bed and pumped into her. Bianca couldn't help but scream, as the new position caused Wise to go even deeper inside her. Bianca had never been fucked so good in her life, and as a tear ran out of one eye, she knew that she was getting close to her climax.

Wise pulled Bianca all the way up, wrapping her arms around his shoulders, before cupping her ass with both of his hands. Finally, Bianca was able to let out a "Fuckkk" before going right back into her moans.

"Yeah, that shit feel good, don't it? A nigga needed this shit right here."

Sweat dripped down both of them, causing their skin to become slippery, but Bianca didn't care. She held onto Wise tightly. When they switched positions and Bianca rode him, the room filled with both their moans. The playlist had long stopped downstairs, but their moans started a new soundtrack. Bianca grinded down, as she looked into Wise's eyes. He cupped her breasts, as her hips moved in circles. Wise leaned up, wrapping Bianca in his stronghold, as she continued to ride him. Their lips collided in a kiss so passionate that it sent both of them into their climax. They both came with the other's name on their lips.

Chapter Six

Bianca woke up wrapped in warm heat. For a moment, she didn't move, just blinked slowly against the soft morning light filtering through the sides of her blackout curtains. Then, she became aware of the arm draped heavily around her waist, the steady breath against the back of her shoulder, and the solid weight of a man's body curled behind hers. Memories from last night rolled in slow, his hands, his mouth, the way he moved inside her for hours. She'd gone from not having sex to getting her back blown out and waking up to him the next morning.

Bianca carefully eased out from under his arm, moving slow enough not to wake him. Her legs felt just a little shaky when she stood, a reminder of what they'd done the night before. She padded into the bathroom, sitting on the toilet and relieving her bladder. When she was done, she brushed her teeth, washed her face, and applied her moisturizer.

She opened the bathroom door and walked back into her room quietly, ready to slip back into bed and pretend she was still asleep. However, she realized that Wise was awake. He sat up against her pillows, covers pooled low around his hips. He lifted his gaze to her, and the corner of his mouth tugged into a slow, sleepy smile.

"Mornin', beautiful."

Bianca froze in the doorway. There was no awkwardness in his voice. He was calm as if right here in her bed was exactly where he was supposed to be. She swallowed, suddenly aware she was standing there naked.

"Good morning," she managed. "There are some extra toothbrushes and face towels in the hall closet right next to the bathroom. It's the last door on the right."

"Thank you," Wise spoke, getting out of bed and walking out of the room.

Bianca sat back on her bed, feeling the emptiness in her stomach after all the liquor she'd consumed the night before. She thought about going to get breakfast but then realized she needed to know when Tasha was coming to pick up her car. Walking downstairs, she grabbed her phone from the table in the living room and placed a call to Tasha, who answered on the second ring.

"Hey, girl. I was just calling to see what time you coming to pick up your car," Bianca said, taking a seat on the couch.

"Bitch, have you not looked outside? It's like two feet of snow out there, and the roads are closed. I can't even leave Marty's house. I should have just went the fuck home last night. It's fuckin' Christmas Eve, and I'm stuck here at this nigga house for I don't know how long. I don't even have shit wrapped yet. How the fuck I'ma explain to the twins that Mama and Santa might not be home for Christmas?"

"Snow? What you talking about?" Bianca asked, getting up from the couch.

When Bianca crossed the room and tugged the curtains open, her breath caught in her throat. A clean, endless blanket of white swallowed everything – cars, curbs, sidewalks, the tops of bushes and hedges. The snow sat high, almost level with the bottom of her porch railing, thick and heavy like someone had poured whipped cream over the whole neighborhood and let it freeze. The street hadn't been plowed yet, not a single tire track, not a footprint, nothing but untouched mounds rolling down the block. The driveway was gone, the walkway was gone, and even the shapes of cars parked on the street were barely recognizable.

"Girl, what the fuck? I didn't even know it had snowed at all, let alone did all this."

Just then, Wise came walking into the living room. "There you are. I thought you'd left me. Do you want to get something to eat before I order an Uber? If you have the stuff, I make a pretty good omelet."

"Girl, where the fuck you at? You not at home either?" Tasha asked through the phone.

"I'm at home. Tasha, let me call you back in a few minutes."

"Call me back? Bianca, who the hell is that man, and where are you?"

"I'm at home, that's Wise, and I'll call you back."

"Oh, bitch, you better. Cause now I got questions."

Before Tasha could say another word, Bianca hung up. She turned to Wise, curtains still open, and pointed out. She didn't panic when she told Wise they were snowed in. She just pulled her robe tighter around herself and shrugged like it was nothing more than an inconvenience. Wise, on the other hand, didn't hide the way his eyebrows lifted.

"For real? Two feet?" he asked, phone already in his hand, as he opened the rideshare app. "Let me see if I can even get an Uber."

"You can try," Bianca replied, walking over to sit back on the couch, "but I doubt anybody's out there driving in all that."

Wise tried anyway. He stood near the window, thumb tapping the screen, staring out at the buried street like he could will a car through the snow. After a few attempts, he slipped the phone into his pocket and exhaled.

"Aight," he said, giving her a small grin. "Let me make us some breakfast while I wait on one of these drivers to get some balls and want some money."

Bianca didn't argue. She just watched him move around her kitchen like he'd been there before, opening cabinets, finding her pans, and cracking eggs into a bowl like it was nothing. The scent of peppers, onions, and butter warmed the air, as he sautéed everything together. She sat on a stool at the island, chin propped in her hand, her eyes following the slow roll of his shoulders.

"Didn't know you could cook," she teased.

"I can do a lil' somethin'. Don't let the baby face fool you," Wise joked, flashing a smile over his shoulder.

He folded the omelets perfectly and slid her plate in front of her before making his own. They ate next to each other at Bianca's kitchen island.

"This is good," Bianca complimented, taking another bite of her omelet.

"Thanks, I'm glad you like it."

After breakfast, Wise grabbed his phone again, checking the app to see if they had located a driver. Bianca stood to her feet, taking the plates over to the sink, and washed them. One hour passed and still not a single car was available. Wise's sigh was heavier this time. He set the phone on the counter and rubbed the back of his neck.

"Still nothing," he confirmed. "Roads must really be shut down."

Bianca nodded, wiping her hands on a towel before meeting his gaze.

"Well," she spoke calmly, "looks like you're stuck with me a little longer."

The way Wise smiled at her words showed her that he didn't mind. She smiled back at him before speaking again.

"Well, I'm about to hop in the shower. When I get out, I can try to find something in my son's old room for you to put on so that you can get in as well."

Wise lifted his chin in acknowledgment, eyes lingering on her just a second too long. "Aight. Do yo' thing."

Bianca headed upstairs, feeling his gaze on her back until she turned the corner. In her bedroom, she moved to her dresser and pulled out something comfortable. She settled on a soft pair of black leggings and an oversized, off the shoulder, cream sweater. She laid the outfit on the bed, grabbed fresh underwear, and headed into the bathroom and turned on the shower. Steam filled the room within minutes, heat rolling over her, as she stepped under the water.

She closed her eyes, letting the water hit the back of her neck. She poured body wash onto her loofah before scrubbing her body down. About ten minutes into her shower, she heard the soft click of the bathroom door opening. Bianca blinked, her heart skipping.

"Wise?" she called over her shoulder, but she already knew it was him.

The shower curtain slid open several inches, letting a rush of cool air in before he stepped through, pulling it closed behind him. Water beaded on his skin instantly, running down the tattoos on his chest, disappearing along the carved lines of muscle. He looked down at her like he wasn't sure if he should speak or touch her first.

"Hope you don't mind," he whispered. "I thought it would be much better if we just took a shower together."

She moved back just enough for him to stand beneath the water with her. His hands went to her waist, warm even under the heat of the shower, and he pulled her closer. He towered over her, as she looked up at him. He leaned down, meeting her halfway, allowing their lips to touch. He kissed her like she was his long lost love, sending chills throughout her body. His lips left hers and began planting a trail of kisses down her neck. She bit her bottom lip, and when Wise cupped her breasts and played with her nipples, she let out a low moan.

Bianca's chest rose and fell in anticipation. His manhood was already rock hard, and Bianca wrapped one hand around it, stroking him, as he fingered her nipples. With her other hand, her fingers traced the back of his neck, as she kissed him deeply. His hands traveled up and down her body, feeling her soft skin. The way he touched her sent lightning bolts through her entire body. Bianca's breath hitched when he turned her around and leaned her over, slapping her ass just enough for it to jiggle.

"Bianca," he whispered, saying her name the moment he inserted himself into her.

Her wetness welcomed the stretch once more, as he filled her up again. Their movements found a rhythm, slow and deep, guided by the water beating down on them and the soft sighs escaping her lips. Wise held her hips securely, biting his bottom lip with each thrust. Bianca couldn't help but notice the difference between last night and now. Wise seemed to move slower and deeper, as if he wanted to show her a different side to his lovemaking.

Wise pulled out slowly before turning Bianca around and lifting her up, pushing her back against the wall. Bianca clung to his shoulders, as she wrapped her legs around him. Her moans were loud, as he reentered her, quickly finding their rhythm again.

"Yeah, this gotta be my pussy. This too good to belong to anyone else," Wise moaned into her ear.

Bianca was lost in so much lust that she would have agreed to damn near anything. So, with that, she agreed to his words.

"This pussy is yours, baby. Can't nobody fuck me like you," she assured.

Just like last night, they came together with each other's names on their lips. Once they finally stepped out of the shower, Bianca wrapped herself in a towel before letting Wise know that she was going to find him something to put on. She slipped out of the bathroom and headed down the hall to Lake's room. She opened his dresser, grabbed a black t-shirt and a pair of gray basketball shorts that looked like they'd fit Wise, then went back to her room where he was waiting on her. He was sitting on the edge of her bed when she returned, towel around his waist, scrolling through his phone. He looked up when she entered, and that slow smile touched his lips again.

"Found you something," Bianca informed, handing him the clothes.

"Good lookin' out," he replied, taking them from her. He stood to his feet, dropping the towel from around his waist, and put on the shorts.

Bianca pulled on her leggings and oversized sweater before sitting cross-legged on the bed. Wise sat beside her, leaning back on his hands, looking even more comfortable than before.

"You good?" he asked, tilting his head toward her.

"Yeah," she replied softly. "Just thinking."

"Thinking about what?"

"You," she admitted before she could second guess it.

Wise smirked. "What about me?"

"Well…" She drew in a deep breath. "For starters, what's your real name? I know Wise ain't on your birth certificate."

He groaned dramatically, dropping his head back. "Man… why you wanna bring that up?"

"Because you been all through my house, my mouth, and my pussy, and I don't even know your real name. I feel like I should at least know that."

Wise sat up and rubbed his palm over his jaw. "Aight. But only 'cause you put it like that. But if you tell anyone, I'm going to deny it." He paused then spoke it quietly. "My name is Myron."

Bianca blinked. "Myron?"

"See, I knew you was gon' be on bullshit. That's why I don't be tellin' nobody."

She hid her laugh behind her hand. "I'm not on bullshit. I promise. I've just never met a Myron before. Like ever."

"That's the problem," he uttered, shaking his head. "It sound like somebody's uncle who fix lawnmowers or some shit. My cousins been calling me Wise since I was like nine. Said I was too grown, always thinkin' like I was an adult. It just stuck with me, and I been Wise ever since."

Bianca nodded slowly, studying him. "You do seem mature for your age. I was surprised when you told me that you were thirty last night."

"Yeah, I get that a lot." He chuckled. "Speaking of last night, I hope you are enjoying our time together as much as I am. I know we kinda stuck together, but to me, it don't feel like that. It's like I would want to be here, even if it wasn't two feet of snow outside."

Bianca blushed. "I can't lie. I wasn't expecting any of this. If

I'm being honest, it's been so long since I'd been with a man that I wasn't even sure I knew how to be with one anymore. But you made me feel different, something I hadn't felt in a long time. I was so heartbroken about my children not being able to come home for Christmas, I didn't even want to go to that damn party. However, Tasha made me. Now, I'm glad that she did because I met you."

"Well, I'm here to tell you that you for sure still got it. That tight muthafucka down there is dangerous. And I'm glad you came to the party too. I know it's Christmas Eve, and you wanted to spend it with your family. But I'm here, and we can still have a wonderful holiday."

"Thank you. You're right. We might as well make the best of this. Who knows how long we gon' be snowed in? I've already bought everything that I need to make Christmas dinner, and I don't want all that food to go to waste. So, later on, we can cook together if you want."

"Yeah, I'm down with that. But what you want to do right now? If your kids were here, what would y'all be doing right now?"

Bianca looked over at the clock on her nightstand and saw that it was a little after two in the afternoon. She paused for a moment, really thinking about what she would be doing at this time if her children were here.

"Well, we would probably be watching *Home Alone* right now. We watch it every year together before me and my daughter start making Christmas dinner. It's their favorite Christmas movie."

"Okay, cool then. We gonna watch *Home Alone.*"

Bianca looked over at him, smiling from ear to ear. "Are you serious?"

"Very. We watching it in the living room or in here?"

"Living room," she confirmed, standing to her feet.

They walked down the stairs, and Bianca told Wise that he could go into the living room and put on the movie, while she went into the kitchen to make the popcorn. When it was done, she poured it into a huge bowl before placing the bowl on the same wooden serving tray that she always used. She added smaller bowls to the tray, but instead of having three, she only needed two. She added the three different popcorn seasonings that she always added to the tray, white cheddar, kettle corn, and movie theater butter. She took two cans of Pepsi from the fridge and put them on the tray before adding Twizzlers, chocolate covered peanuts, and chocolate covered pretzels as well. It was the same assortment of snacks her and her children had every year, while they watched the movie. However, this year, she would be watching the movie with Wise.

She walked over to the living room, holding the tray of goodies, and set them on the coffee table in front of them.

"Damn, all this for one movie? You tryna spoil me or something?" he teased.

"Boy, it's popcorn and a few snacks. This the same set up we have every year." Bianca laughed, grabbing the two smaller bowls, filling them with popcorn, and handing one to Wise.

She grabbed all three seasoning flavors before sitting on the couch next to Wise. She put her feet up on the couch and grabbed the fluffy blanket from behind her. She put the blanket over her and Wise, cuddling up close to him. He slid an arm around her shoulders as if he'd been doing it for years, pulling her into his side. Bianca didn't even hesitate, as she relaxed into his warmth. His body was solid and comfortable, as she snuggled up. She grabbed the remote and pressed play on the movie.

They ate popcorn, as the movie played, laughing at the funny parts. Halfway through the movie, Wise leaned up and grabbed both cans of Pepsi, handing one to Bianca. She took it, smiling, and thanked him. She couldn't help but to think about how sweet it was that he wanted to make her Christmas Eve feel as normal as possible. It was hard for her to accept the fact that neither one of her children were here. And although she would have rather it be them there, she couldn't deny the smile he'd put on her face.

"What I don't understand is how they left him alone anyway. Like y'all had one job, and that was to be a parent to the children you had. You mean to tell me they was so worried about catchin' a damn flight that they would leave they own son? That shit is crazy to me," Wise spoke.

"Yeah, and they did it twice. Don't forget in part two, he was lost in New York."

"See what I mean? They ain't need to be parents. But if you want, we can watch part two and talk about their bad parenting later," Wise joked.

Bianca smiled, grabbing the remote and putting on the next movie. Her phone rang, and she looked down at the screen, seeing that it was Tasha. She silenced it, knowing there was no way she was coming to pick up her car today. She placed her can of pop on the end table next to the couch before tugging the blanket over her shoulder and snuggling a little closer to Wise.

Chapter Seven

The credits rolled up the screen, *as Home Alone 2* ended, but neither Bianca nor Wise moved right away. They stayed tucked together on the couch, sharing the last bit of popcorn, letting the warmth between them stretch out. Finally, Bianca exhaled and sat up a little.

"Well... I guess I should start on Christmas dinner. That's usually what I would do after the movie. Me and my daughter would head to the kitchen and start cooking."

He laughed. "Oh, so you sayin' you tryna put me to work?"

"I'm absolutely tryna put you to work," she teased, grabbing his hand and pulling him off the couch. "Come on."

They walked into the kitchen, and Bianca turned on the lights before she began wiping down the counters. She washed her hands then walked over to the refrigerator and began pulling out items, placing them onto the counter. She noticed Wise looking at her, smiling, as he watched her every move.

"Why you looking at me like that?"

"I'm just watching. Seeing you in your element. What all we cooking tonight?"

"Dressing, macaroni and cheese, greens, yams, pasta salad, and seasoning the meat. All the meat gonna get cooked in the morning, along with the twice baked potatoes and garden salads."

"Damn, and what's the meat?"

"Turkey, fried chicken, and lamb chops."

Wise blinked. "You do all that by yourself every year?"

Bianca looked back at him with a small smile. "It's Christmas, so you're supposed to have a huge meal. My daughter and I usually do it together, but this year, I seem to have you."

"Alright then. Put me where you need me," Wise replied.

"If you want, you can start by cutting the onions, peppers, and celery. After that, you can peel and cut the sweet potatoes."

"I'm on it," Wise replied, washing his hands.

Bianca walked over to her small speaker on the counter and pressed play. The soft opening of Mint Condition's *U Send Me Swingin'* floated into the room, and Wise instantly smiled.

"Oh, yeah, this the vibe right here."

Bianca swayed her hips to the beat, as she filled a pot with water. "I gotta have my music playin'. If I don't, my food not gon' come out right."

"That's funny. My mama used to say the same thing."

"That shit is true. Real cooks know it."

Bianca placed the pot on the stove and turned it on. As she waited for the water to boil, she grabbed two wine glasses from the cabinet and filled them with a chilled white wine she'd gotten from the fridge. She then handed one of the glasses off to Wise. She took a sip before she began picking and cleaning collard greens. Wise sat at her kitchen island, chopping onions, and peppers as he sang along to Groove Theory.

"Make sure you chop up a lot of onions because I need them for a lot of the things I'm going to make."

"I got you," he assured.

Bianca continued with the greens, and once they were all chopped and cleaned, she seasoned the water before putting her turkey necks inside. She then placed another pan on the stove and turned it on before melting butter inside. She began sautéing onions and greens before placing in the pot with the turkey necks. She then moved on to making the cornbread for her dressing.

They moved around each other easily, sipping on wine and singing along to songs, as they cooked together.

"This is my very first time cooking a Christmas dinner," Wise admitted. "I ain't gonna lie. I never even wanted to help my mama and aunts cook. And to be honest, they probably wouldn't have let me."

"I'll let you in on a little something too. This my first time cooking Christmas dinner with anyone other than my daughter. I like this." Bianca smiled.

"I know you're sad that we got all this snow, and they couldn't come. But I hope that I'm making this a good holiday for you under the circumstances."

Bianca nodded her head, letting Wise know that he was. They continued cooking, moving onto the macaroni and cheese. Bianca let him know that she must have thought he was special if she was allowing him to be in her kitchen, while she made the dish, letting Wise know that her macaroni recipe was top secret. Wise laughed it off but was sure to take a mental note of how she prepared it. *Making Love* by Keith Sweat came on, and Wise froze.

"Oh, this my shit right here. This shit gon' have me movin' this food and fuckin' you right here on this kitchen island."

Bianca stirred the noodles, cheeks warming, as she blushed. "Don't start that right now. As much as I would love for that to happen, I have to finish this dinner."

"Why does it matter what time we get done cooking? We the only ones eating this, so it don't matter what time dinner is tomorrow."

"Well, if you want to eat dinner at all tomorrow, then I gotta finish cooking it."

Wise smiled, nodding his head and throwing his hands up. "You right. We can finish cooking first. We got all night for dessert."

Bianca shook her head and laughed. However, the truth was, she couldn't wait for the food to finish cooking. She loved the way Wise felt in and on her body. She didn't know what it was about him, but he made her feel different. Even though they had only known each other for a few short hours, the chemistry they had was undeniable. It was almost as if Wise was the missing puzzle piece that Bianca had been searching for all this time.

Opening the cabinet, she grabbed three huge plastic bowls. She then grabbed the meat, lemons, and vinegar and began washing the meat thoroughly. When it was all clean and dry, Wise marinated the lamb chops, while Bianca seasoned the turkey and chicken wings. By the time they finished prepping everything, the once clean kitchen now looked like a disaster but smelled amazing. Bianca leaned against the counter with her wine glass, breathing in the familiar aroma that now truly smelled like Christmas.

"This was fun," he spoke quietly.

"Yeah," she admitted. "It was. Now we gotta clean all this shit up."

"It's all good. That's the easy part for me. I'll wash, and you can dry."

Bianca looked up at him, nodding her head. "That sounds like a plan. Let me grab another bottle of wine first."

They cleaned and sipped, singing along to R&B the entire time. By the time the last pot was washed and the counters were wiped down, Bianca's kitchen was back sparkling again. She dried her hands on a towel and leaned against the counter, watching Wise, as he downed the rest of the wine in his glass.

"I bought some board games," she uttered casually. "Stuff for me and the kids to play tonight. We could break one out if you want to."

Wise made a face instantly. "I ain't really a board game kinda dude."

Bianca laughed. "Oh, okay, that's cool."

"But..." he added, pointing at her. "If you got a deck of cards, that's different."

Her eyebrow lifted. "Oh, yeah?"

"Yeah. We can get a card game going."

She pushed off the counter. "I know I got some somewhere."

She disappeared into the hallway and came back a moment later holding up a worn deck of cards. "Found them."

Wise's grin spread slow and wicked. "That's what's up. Let's do this shit."

They settled at the dining table with their second bottle of wine almost empty and a third bottle right next to it. Bianca shuffled the cards, while Wise explained the rules of Tonk.

"Loser gotta pay up though," he added.

"Pay how?" she asked, already suspicious.

He took a sip of wine. "We gotta make it interesting."

She narrowed her eyes. "Define interesting."

Wise leaned back in his chair. "Strip Tonk. Lose a hand, lose an article of clothing."

Bianca laughed out loud. "Boy, you crazy."

"What's wrong? You scared? You just had that little pussy all in my mouth, so don't act like you scared for me to see it now," he teased.

She picked up her cards and met his gaze. "Please, I ain't never scared. You, on the other hand, should be."

She shuffled the cards before allowing Wise to cut the deck. The truth was she hadn't played Tonk in years. However, there was no way she was going to allow anyone to challenge her and she not accept it. She took another sip from her glass before they started the game. Wise lost the first hand and tossed his t-shirt over the chair without hesitation. Bianca clapped dramatically, laughing at Wise sitting there shirtless.

Wise dealt the next hand, while Bianca opened the third bottle of wine and refilled their glasses. Bianca lost the next round, slipping out of her shirt and folding it neatly like she wasn't affected at all. Wise's eyes lingered just a beat before he burst into laughter.

"Not you foldin' that shit up all nice and neat."

"Well, excuse me for wanting to keep my things together neatly."

"Just keep playin'. You gon' be folding more of yo' shit up," Wise joked.

They continued to play, and Wise lost the next round. He removed one of his socks and placed it on top of the shirt he'd already taken off. Bianca looked at him with a smirk but didn't say anything. Although she was winning at the moment, she knew it was still anybody's game, and the tables could turn just as quickly. The music still played, and she tapped her manicured finger on her glass, as she sang and waited for Wise to deal the next hand. Coincidentally, that was also the hand that Bianca lost. Standing up, she slid out of her pants, folding them and placing them on top of her shirt.

Wise exhaled under his breath. "Damn. You tryna make a nigga hard, my baby?"

"This strippin' shit was your idea. Just focus on the game," she warned, settling back into her chair.

The third bottle of wine was almost gone, and Bianca had just lost the next hand. She paused, looking down at the cards as if she couldn't believe he'd won again. Once she studied the cards and was sure he'd actually won that hand, she nodded slowly. She reached behind her back and unclasped her bra, letting it slide off her shoulders, then pulled it off slowly, exposing her full breasts.

Wise swallowed hard, shaking his head slowly. "This ain't fair. How am I supposed to pay attention to my cards when you sitting there like that? All I wanna do is come over there and suck on them muthafuckas."

"You suggested it, so figure it out. But I know one thing. Ain't nothing getting sucked until after I see who wins this game."

He laughed softly, rubbing his jaw. "Damn, you competitive, lil baby."

"And you better know it. You challenged me, so now we gotta complete it." She smiled. "Your deal," she continued.

Wise picked up the deck, hands steady, as he shuffled them. They finally called game when Wise lost his last hand. He stood slowly, completely unbothered, stepping out of the last piece of clothing. Bianca's breath hitched despite herself. She leaned back in her chair, braless now, still in her panties, wine glass dangling loosely from her fingers.

"I guess you won because I'm standing here naked as hell," Wise joked. "What you wanna do next? You still bake cookies for Santa?"

Bianca laughed softly. "I haven't done that in years. My kids grew up and stopped believing in Santa. But we could bake some if you want to. I got some chocolate chip cookie dough in the fridge."

Wise walked over to her, putting one hand on the table and leaning down in front of her. His mouth hovered over hers, like he wanted to kiss her but was holding back. Her nipples hardened, as she looked into his eyes.

"Nah," he whispered. "All I really need is some milk."

Her pulse jumped at his words. Before she could reply, his hand slid up her thigh slowly, his touch sending shivers down her spine. His hand landed at the top of her lace panties, and she licked her lips. Bianca swallowed, fingers curling into the fabric of the chair, as Wise slipped his hand inside her panties and found her love button. The room seemed to tilt slightly, and soft moans escaped her lips.

"I already have all the cookies I need right here," he whispered. "How 'bout we go upstairs, so I can eat it?"

Chapter Eight

They walked into the room, heat already pooling between Bianca's legs. This entire time had felt like a movie to her. *What are the odds I meet a man at a party that I didn't even want to go to and end up getting put through the mattress for two days straight?* Wise pulled Bianca into him, rubbing his hands down her back and over her ass. His fingertips ran up her hips, over her stomach, and up the curve of her breast before finally resting on the bottom of her chin, tilting it upward and bringing her into a kiss. Her legs became weak, and her knees trembled.

Without a word, Wise lifted Bianca into his arms and carried her over to her dresser, her hand sliding down his brawn shoulders before roaming over his abs. He stood between her legs with his erect manhood pressed against her stomach. He broke the kiss slowly before dropping to his knees and draping one of her legs over his shoulder. She felt his lips first, as he planted gentle kisses between her thighs and on her love box. Bianca closed her eyes, letting the feeling take over. Her body responded before her mind could catch up, her hips lifting slightly, as her fingers gripped the edge of the dresser.

Bianca hissed when Wise's tongue flicked over her, tasting her juices. Her eyes rolled into the back of her head. *Fuck, it feels so good. I ain't never in my life had my pussy ate like this,* she thought, as she grinded slowly against his mouth. Her thoughts fractured when Wise slid two fingers inside her wetness.

"Auhhh, fuck!" she moaned. "Yesss, right there. Just like that."

Her breath hitched, as the dual sensation deepened. His fingers seemed to be making a mess that his tongue was cleaning up. She felt the heat curl low in her belly, spreading outward, making her toes curl and her shoulders tense before dropping again. His name slipped from her lips without permission, soft and breathless. Her hands slid into his hair, holding his tongue in a spot that had her questioning every oral experience she'd ever had. Every second felt intentional, like his tongue was telling her something that he didn't have the words to say.

"I could eat this shit for hours. I ain't never ate a pussy as sweet as yours," Wise spoke between licks.

With those words, Bianca's legs began to shake uncontrollably, as her climax neared. Her moans became louder, and she grabbed one of her breasts just as she erupted into Wise's mouth. When she finally opened her eyes, her gaze met his. They didn't speak, just looked at each other for several seconds, before Wise leaned in and kissed her on the lips. Slowly, he lifted her off of the dresser before leading her over to her bed. They stopped at the foot, Bianca's hands tracing the lines in his abs. He kissed her softly before lifting her up and laying Bianca on the bed. Their bodies aligned naturally, like they'd already figured out how to fit.

Wise leaned down and kissed Bianca again, this time longer but softer, a kiss that sent tingles through Bianca's entire body. Her hands slid up his arms, up his shoulders, and to his face, holding him in place, as they kissed. Her body responded without thought, hips shifting slightly, breath turning uneven. She felt awake in a way she hadn't in years, and she knew it was all because of him. He broke their kiss, and his lips found her neck, as he pushed into her slowly. He didn't rush. Every move he made was intentional, and Bianca knew it.

She arched into him, fingers clutching his shoulders, her breath breaking softly into the quiet room. The pleasure built gradually, like a rising tide. Her name slipped from his lips, low and muffled from his mouth being buried in her neck, but she heard it. She spread her thighs wider and allowed Wise to go deeper into her.

"Damn, you gon' fuck around and make a nigga fall in love if you keep givin' me this pussy. It's so tight," he moaned, this time into her ear.

He pumped in and out of her slowly. Bianca didn't know why, but this time felt different than the other times they'd had sex. It was softer and more sensual. His thrusts were deeper, and his touch was even more gentle than before. If Bianca didn't know any better, she would think he was making love to her. She felt the warmth in her chest, and when Wise picked his head up just enough to make eye contact with her, she saw the look in his eyes. It didn't lie, rather confirmed what Bianca already expected. Right there, in her bed, with their bodies tangled together, they were making love.

"Say you promise, and I'll give it to you every day." The words slipped out before she even realized what she was saying.

However, once she'd spoke them, she knew she meant them. She wrapped her legs around his waist, moving her hips slowly and matching his rhythm. It was as if in that very moment, they'd become one. She didn't know how they'd gotten here and so fast, but she welcomed it, wanting to know where they would go from here. They came together with each other's names on their lips.

Wise didn't move for a moment after they came. Instead, he stayed inside her, breathing heavy, as he held onto her tightly. It was almost as if he thought she would disappear if he didn't hold her tightly. Bianca didn't mind. In fact, she welcomed it, holding onto him just as tightly. When Wise finally pulled out of her, he laid next to her, pulling her close. They didn't speak. There was no need to. Everything was already understood in the way Wise held her. They fell asleep with Bianca wrapped in Wise's arms.

Bianca's eyes fluttered open to the softest brush of lips against her neck. Her body stirred instinctively, and a small smile tugged at her lips. The sunlight streaming through the curtains lit the room with an early morning glow. Wise's lips were warm against her skin, and she tilted her head a bit so that she could look at him.

"Merry Christmas," Wise whispered against her skin.

"Merry Christmas," Bianca murmured, turning toward him to press a soft kiss to his lips.

"I can't believe I'm still here," Wise spoke, his forehead resting against hers. "Not in a bad way. It's just that things like this don't happen in real life. And now after spending the last two days with you, my feelings all caught up in this shit."

Bianca laughed softly, brushing a strand of hair from her face. It was then that she realized she'd went to sleep without her bonnet on, and her hair must have looked crazy. However, Wise didn't seem to care, still looking at her like she was the most beautiful woman in the world.

"I'm glad you're here. You made these last two days way better than I thought it would be. Who knew that a snowstorm would end up like this? I thought my Christmas was ruined, but you showed me that even though things don't go as planned, the outcome can still be great. Thank you for that."

Wise grinned, his eyes never leaving hers. "You're welcome, but in reality, I should be thanking you."

Bianca nodded her head before sliding out of bed. After a quick trip to the bathroom to pee, brush her teeth, and wash her face, Bianca returned to find Wise sitting on the edge of the bed. Bianca walked over to her windows, opening her curtains and allowing the natural light to shine into the room.

"You ready for breakfast?" Bianca asked, looking back at Wise.

Wise nodded his head before standing to his feet. They walked downstairs, and Bianca opened all the curtains before finally walking into the kitchen. She pulled out ingredients for cinnamon rolls, eggs, and bacon, and Wise rolled up his sleeves, immediately jumping in to help. They moved around the kitchen together naturally, as if they had been doing it for years. Wise flipped the bacon, while Bianca pulled the cinnamon rolls from the oven. When the food was ready, they sat at Bianca's kitchen island, plates of food in front of them. The scent of sugar, cinnamon, and bacon were in the air, but Bianca's focus was mostly on him.

Wise leaned back, stretching his arms. "Bianca, this is so nice. I never even had breakfast on Christmas morning, not even as a kid. I didn't even know this was even a thing."

Bianca stopped mid bite and looked up at him. "What do you mean you never had Christmas breakfast? What did y'all eat on Christmas morning then?"

"We didn't eat nothing on Christmas morning. We got up and opened gifts. Then, we played with whatever we had until it was time to get dressed to go to my aunt's house. Usually, the first meal I have on Christmas day is Christmas dinner."

"Wow, now I didn't know that was a thing. We've always had Christmas breakfast. Even when I was a kid, my mama would always get up Christmas morning and cook a huge breakfast before she finished cooking dinner."

After breakfast, they cleaned the kitchen together, Wise washing the dishes while Bianca dried. Then, it was time to finish preparing Christmas dinner. The house filled with the smell of fried chicken, lamb chops, and turkey. Every so often, their fingers brushed or their eyes met. About two hours later, everything was either in the oven or simmering on the stove. Bianca leaned against the counter, sipping from a cup of coffee and watching Wise wash his hands at her kitchen sink. She watched closely, as his bare muscles flexed when he dried his hands with a paper towel.

"What do you usually do now, while you wait on the food to finish cooking?" Wise asked.

"Well, we would probably be in the living room opening gifts and listening to Christmas music. I would have the fireplace lit, and they would probably be thanking me for everything I got them," Bianca replied.

Wise smiled at her before taking her hand and leading her to the living room. The snow outside was still white and beautiful and still was not plowed yet. In reality, the city probably wouldn't have any workers come out until the day after Christmas. The truth was, Bianca didn't mind being snowed in with Wise. She was actually enjoying it. She was so sad before, thinking that this would be the worst Christmas she'd ever had. She thought she would be spending it alone. However, this was turning out to be one of the best times of her life. She took her seat on the couch, while Wise walked over to the fireplace. She watched as he placed the wood inside and lit it.

She heard the crackle of the fire before she felt the warmth. She pulled the blanket over her legs just as Wise walked over to the couch and took his seat next to her. He wrapped his arm around her, and she leaned her head on his shoulder. They sat there, watching the fire, and the way the snow was piled outside the window looked like a Christmas card. Wise looked over at Bianca with a smile on his face.

"Why you looking at me like that?"

"Nothing, I just think it's time to bring you in on one of my Christmas traditions."

"Oh, okay." Bianca shifted, turning to give Wise her full attention. "Okay, I'm all ears. What we 'bout to do?"

"We are about to watch my all-time favorite Christmas movie. I have been watching it on Christmas day since I was a kid, and I never go a Christmas without it."

"Well, let's watch it. I never need an excuse to watch a Christmas movie. What's your favorite?"

"*A Christmas Story*. Not only do I watch it every year, but it plays all day on the TV in my house on Christmas day."

Bianca laughed before handing Wise the remote. He went through every streaming service Bianca had until he finally found the movie and pressed play. Wise watched it like he'd never seen it before, and Bianca watched him in amusement, as he cracked up at the movie like it was the funniest thing he'd ever seen. Halfway through the movie, Bianca's phone rang. Looking down at the screen, she saw it was Tasha. Wise paused the movie just as Bianca swiped the talk button.

"Merry Christmas," Bianca answered cheerfully.

"Well, Merry Christmas to you too. You sound so much better. I know the kids ain't made it in all this snow. What got you so cheerful this morning? Let me find out you been getting that back blown out," Tasha joked.

"And have," Bianca replied with a smile.

"Ohhhh, shit, bitch. I need every single detail. I knew once I heard his voice in the background yesterday that Stella had finally got her groove back. Where is he now?"

"Please, Tasha." Bianca laughed. "He's right here. We in the living room watching his favorite Christmas movie."

"Oh, y'all doing relationship shit. That was quick, but I love that for you. I ain't gonna hold you up. I just wanted to check in on you and make sure you wasn't up under the bed crying. I see he got you together though."

"Yeah, he did," Bianca replied, looking over at Wise with a smile.

Bianca placed her phone back on the end table before curling back up next to Wise. He pressed play, and they continued to watch the movie. When it was over, Bianca walked into the kitchen to check on the turkey. Her phone rang again, and she rushed over to it, looking down at it. She smiled when she saw Journey's picture flashing.

"Merry Christmas, baby girl," Bianca answered. "How are you today?"

"Merry Christmas, Mommy. I'm okay. How are you?"

"I'm good, just snowed in. But it's all good. I'm cooking Christmas dinner and just chillin'. I wish you and your brother could have came, but everything will still be here when y'all get here. I'll just have to cook again. But we can have Christmas when y'all are able to fly in. What are you doing today?"

"Yeah, we can do that. Hopefully, I'll be able to fly in next week before New Year's Eve. Today, I'm going over one of my friend's house. She's having Christmas dinner for everyone in our friend group that wasn't able to go home for the holiday."

"Oh, that's good. I'm glad you have something to do and ain't just gonna be in your dorm alone."

They talked for about twenty minutes before they ended the call, and Bianca walked back into the living room. Wise was still on the couch, watching *A Christmas Story* for the second time. Bianca laughed and sat next to him on the couch.

"You wasn't playing when you said it played all day long at your house, huh?"

"Nope, I don't lie. This my shit, but since we at your house, we can turn it off and watch something else if you want to."

Bianca grabbed the remote and began going through movies. When she found *Four Christmases*, her face lit up. The moment that Wise told her he'd never seen it, she knew that would be their next movie. By the time the credits were rolling, Bianca was back in the kitchen, basting the turkey. She knew that once it was done, dinner would be ready, and they could eat. She was just about to go into her room and find something to put on when her phone rang. She looked down, smiling, when she saw it was Lake. She answered cheerfully, telling her son Merry Christmas. She became even more cheerful when Lake told her that he was able to switch his flight and would be home for New Years as long as the weather allowed it. When she ended the call, she was all smiles at the way her holiday had done an entire one eighty.

Chapter Nine

By late afternoon, everything was ready and inside the serving trays. Bianca had set the food up on a long table in her dining room as if it were a buffet. There was so much food, you would have thought Bianca had cooked for an army instead of just the two of them. She stood in her bedroom, towel wrapped around her body, water droplets still on her shoulder from the shower. She reached into her closet and pulled out the outfit she'd planned to wear, a deep emerald-green, knit dress, soft and fitted but not tight. It had long sleeves that hugged her arms and fell just below her knees. She paired it with black ankle boots and a pair of small gold hoops with a matching necklace and bracelet.

Once she was dressed, she walked over to her dresser to select her fragrance of the day. She wanted something that was warm and sexy but not too much. She chose Maison Margiela Replica By The Fireplace. She sprayed herself before fixing her hair. She looked at herself in the mirror one last time, liking what she saw. She was comfortable yet still cute enough for Christmas dinner.

Wise was already in the hallway when she stepped out the room. He stopped when he saw her, smiling, as he looked her up and down.

"Damn," he said softly, not trying to hide it. "You look amazing."

Bianca laughed under her breath. "Thank you. Come on, let's go into Lake's room so you can get something to wear. I got him a new pack of underwear that you can just have because I know you need some."

"Thank you."

They walked into Lake's room together, Bianca going directly to his closet. She selected a crisp black button-up and a pair of black slacks. She tossed in a belt and a clean pair of socks before walking out of the room, allowing him to get dressed. While he changed, she stepped back into the kitchen, taking plates from the cabinet. She'd bought plates especially for today, matching the décor throughout the house perfectly. When Wise returned, she turned and smiled at the way Lake's clothes fit him perfectly.

"You clean up nice," Bianca complimented.

"Thank you. Do you need help with anything?"

"Yeah, can you grab those plates right there?" She pointed. "We're going to eat in the dining room, and I need to set the table."

He grabbed the plates, while Bianca grabbed the utensils and cloth napkins, and they made their way into the dining room. She set the table, laying each plate down carefully before neatly folding the napkins. She placed the utensils next to the plates before lighting the candles that she'd placed in the center of the table. Wise watched her for a moment before speaking.

"You didn't have to do all this. It's just us."

"Yes, I did. It's Christmas," she replied simply.

They filled their plates and sat across from one another at the table. Bianca asked Wise to bless the food, and they bowed their heads, while he did so. They held conversation, as they enjoyed the meal. They spoke about childhood and past Christmases they remembered, as well as their futures. Wise told Bianca that he hoped this was just one of the many times they would be seeing each other. He let her know that he hoped this was just the start of their relationship.

"I hope it is too. I've really been enjoying the time we've been spending together."

"Me too. And you can cook. Shit, I'ma fuck around and never want to leave."

"Let me find out you want this forever. I might not be mad at that," she joked.

"Shit. Let me find out you don't mind."

They continued to talk and eat, and when dinner was over, Bianca brought in the pecan pie she'd purchased from the store. She cut them both a slice, and she sat back down at the table. When they were done, Wise helped her carry the plates to the kitchen before they rinsed them off and loaded her dishwasher. She leaned back against the counter for a moment, exhaling. The house was clean, and the food was put away. Wise stood a few feet away, drying his hands with a paper towel before throwing it away.

"This turned out to be an amazing day," Wise spoke. "I know I keep saying that, but it's the truth. I'm so glad that I ended up spending my Christmas with you."

Bianca smiled. "Yeah, it really did. I had no idea it would be like this. I thought I would be sad and lonely. But you lifted my spirits, amongst other things." She winked.

They both laughed, and Bianca grabbed a bottle of wine from her counter, this time a red blend. She took two glasses out of the cabinet. After opening the bottle, she poured wine into both glasses and handed one to Wise.

"Oh, you tryna have a redo of last night? Let me find out you wanna break out the cards again," Wise joked, taking the glass from her.

"I mean, it's Christmas. I feel like it's only right to drink on Christmas and New Year's Eve." She smiled, taking a sip from her glass.

She turned off the kitchen light, and the house softened immediately. The only light was the glow of the Christmas tree coming in from the living room. Bianca walked over to Wise, taking his hand into hers and motioning for him to follow her. They moved to the living room together hand in hand. Wise sat first, stretching his legs out. Bianca curled up beside him, tucking her feet beneath her, leaning into the corner of the couch. Wise rested his arm along the back of the couch, and Bianca felt the heat of his body.

Bianca reached for the remote and muted the TV. *A Christmas Story* had been playing on repeat per Wise's request. And although she was going to let the movie play, she didn't feel the need to keep hearing it. Instead, she turned on an old school R&B playlist. Tevin Campbell's *I'm Ready* came through the speakers, and Wise instantly began singing.

"Oh, this yo' shit, huh?"

Wise nodded his head yes, still singing and looking Bianca directly in her eyes.

Bianca smiled, realizing that he was singing to her. He stood to his feet, holding his hand out for her to take. He pulled her up from the couch, wrapping his arms around her waist, as he pulled her closer to him. They danced slowly, as Wise continued to sing softly. When the song went off, Wise kissed Bianca on her forehead before pulling back a little. Picking his glass up from the table, Wise drank it before walking into the kitchen and retrieving the bottle. He refilled both of their glasses before changing the song on the radio.

"What's a Detroit party without a few hustles?" Wise asked, turning on *The Turbo Hustle.*

Bianca smiled "Oh, you tryna party party. You ain't say all that."

Bianca took a quick sip of her wine before putting her glass down on the coffee table. They began moving their feet to the directions in the song, laughing and smiling, as they danced. When that was over, *The Freak Beats Hustle* came on right after. The Christmas tree lights blinked rhythmically, casting gentle shadows across the room, as they danced. When the *Tamia Shuffle* came on, Bianca grabbed her glass off the table and took her seat on the couch.

"What you doing? You done dancing?" Wise asked, confused.

"Boy, I don't know this one. I can't get nothing after she say, 'when I think about you.' After that, I'm lost."

"That's the beginning of the damn song." Wise laughed.

"Exactly. And that is probably the only hustle I don't know. I hope I ain't done put my city to shame."

"You not because I'm about to teach you the hustle. Come on."

Bianca shook her head but still stood to her feet after taking another sip from her glass. Wise started slow, showing her each step with a count. Bianca watched his feet, studying them and trying to memorize each step. When he started the song over, he asked Bianca to try. She took a few steps then stumbled, damn near falling flat on her face. They both laughed before Bianca tried again. After about the fifth try, Bianca finally got it, and they danced through the entire song together. When the next song came on, the tempo switched, slowing. Wise smiled, grabbing Bianca's waist, as Donny Hathaway's *A Song For You* played through the speakers. They danced slow, Wise's hands firm against her body. She rested her head on his chest, as they continued to dance.

They stayed like that their bodies pressed against each other. Until Bianca finally pulled back, looking up at him. Wise leaned down, kissing her lips gently. He moved his kisses from her lips to her neck. She moaned softly, as his tongue moved in gentle circles. His hands trailed up her body, pulling her dress with them.

"I think it's time you let me unwrap my gift," Wise whispered.

He pulled her dress over her head and dropped it to the floor. She stood there in her olive-green bra and panties set. Wise moved, reaching for the blanket that was on the couch. He laid it down carefully on the floor in front of the tree. Bianca allowed him to guide her to the blanket, her body relaxing as soon as her back met the softness beneath her. Wise knelt between her legs, slow and deliberate, pulling her panties off slowly. She watched as he leaned down, positioning himself between her thighs.

She felt the warm heat of his mouth instantly, as his tongue moved up and down her slit. She gasped softly, fingers gripping the blanket beneath her, as a low moan escaped her lips. Wise smiled against her skin, clearly pleased by the way her body reacted so instinctively to him.

"Relax," he murmured.

She did, letting go of thought, control, and everything else that wasn't Wise's tongue. His tongue worked in slow strokes, firm and wet. Her breaths became uneven, as she unraveled beneath him. Bianca pressed her hand to his head, holding him there, not wanting him to stop. He kissed and licked until Bianca couldn't take anymore, and her juices ran into his mouth. When he finally rose back up to her, Bianca pulled him close without a word, her arms wrapping around his neck. She kissed him deeply, unhurried, letting him feel exactly how affected she was from the feeling he'd given her.

Wise rolled off of her, lying next to her and wrapping his arm around her. However, Bianca wasn't done. Rolling over, she scooted down, hovering over his manhood, before taking him into her mouth. Wise hissed as Bianca sucked, sending loud slurping noises over the music already playing. He allowed his hand to travel to her head and grip a handful of her hair. She didn't stop him; instead, she sucked fasted. She looked up at him, watching the facial expression he made.

She sucked for a few more minutes before taking him out of her mouth and sitting up and straddling him. She eased down on him, taking him inside her. She rode him slowly, moving her hips in slow circles. Wise gripped her ass, as she bit her bottom lip.

"Damn, baby. You riding this muthafucka. Fuckkk, just like that," Wise coached.

Bianca continued to ride him, as their moans filled the room. They stayed in that position until they both came. Bianca slid off of him slowly and laid beside him on the blanket. She rested her head against Wise's shoulder then shifted closer, her cheek settling against his chest. His arm draped around her, wrapping her in comfort.

They stayed on the floor longer than either of them realized, the music drifting through the room. Bianca traced absent patterns along Wise's chest. Outside, the white blanket of snow still covered the ground, but Bianca had never felt warmer.

Wise broke the silence first. "Can I tell you something?" he asked, looking down at her.

She hummed softly in response, eyes still closed.

"I didn't think today would be like this," he revealed. "When I woke up yesterday morning and saw all the snow outside, I thought maybe it would feel awkward. But it didn't. It actually felt natural and easy, like this is where I was supposed to be."

"Yeah, I get what you're saying. I thought the same thing, but it turned out perfect."

They shifted, eventually moving back to the couch, pulling the blanket with them. Bianca tucked her feet beneath her again, instinctively finding the same position she always did. Wise leaned back, stretching his legs out, pulling her gently into his side. Bianca rested her head against his shoulder and stared at the tree. The lights blinked slowly, reflecting off the ornaments. They sat on the couch, cuddled up next to each other, not speaking, just enjoying each other and the music that played.

"So, what's next after this?" Bianca asked, finally breaking the silence.

"What do you mean? Shit, we can do anything you want to do. I'm open to whatever," Wise replied.

"I mean with us. What's next? When this snow clears then what?"

Wise shifted, positioning himself so that he was eye to eye with her. Bianca looked up at him, as she waited on his response. She looked into his eyes, trying to read him, before he opened his mouth to answer.

"Well, if it's up to me, then I don't want this to end. I feel like I found something special in you, and I want to see where this could go. I feel like I've been waiting on you my entire life, and I want to know if that's true."

Bianca smiled, glad that they felt the same way about each other. "I would like that too," she replied.

She leaned forward, kissing his lips, before resting her forehead against his chest. For a moment, she just took it all in, the heartbreak that turned into happiness. She'd thought this would be a lonely Christmas, but instead, she now thought she may have found a long-term partner in life. Love hadn't been good to her throughout the years, but she hoped Wise would change all that.

He looked down at her, kissing her forehead. "You ready for bed?" he asked softly.

"Yeah," she replied. "I think I am."

Bianca locked her arm around his, and they walked up to her room, leaving the lights on the Christmas tree glowing. They settled in the bed, and Wise pulled her close to him, as they wrapped the covers over their bodies. Bianca tucked herself against him, fitting easily and comfortably. For the first time in a long time, she felt safe. As Bianca drifted toward sleep, one thought settled gently into her mind. She wasn't lonely at all this Christmas; she'd found someone to share it with. And she hoped that it would be the start of many more together.

Epilogue

ONE YEAR LATER

Bianca opened her eyes to the sun peeking in through the curtains. For a moment, she just laid there. It was Christmas morning, and the house was quiet. The air smelled like a mix of apple cinnamon and vanilla. Bianca smiled to herself. She pushed the covers back and padded into the bathroom, the tile cool beneath her feet. She used the bathroom, relieving her bladder, before washing her hands. The red silk Christmas pajamas felt good against her skin. Once she brushed her teeth and washed her face, she studied her reflection in the mirror. Although she was tired from all the cooking she'd done the night before, she couldn't stop the smile that spread across her face.

When she opened the bathroom door and stepped back into the hallway, the smell of coffee hit her nose. Bianca moved slowly down the hall, passing framed photos that hung on the wall – one of Journey when she graduated high school and another one of Lake from when he graduated college. She stopped in front of the closed door and reached for the knob. She smiled as she walked into the nursery.

Soft morning light spilled through cream-colored curtains, warming the room. The walls were painted a gentle blush with hints of gray. A plush, light pink rug covered the floor, clouds stitched into its surface. Two white cribs sat side by side, close enough that the babies could sense each other even in sleep. Wise was already inside the nursery. He stood near the window, one twin cradled carefully in his arms, as he fed her a bottle. Bianca's heart swelled, as she walked over to him. Wise turned, smiling, when he saw Bianca.

"Good morning, baby. Merry Christmas," he greeted.

"Merry Christmas to you too. Did she eat yet?" Bianca asked, pointing over at the other crib.

"She just finished."

Bianca smiled. "Merry first Christmas, Sage," she cooed, kissing Sage's forehead gently.

She then walked over to the other crib where Sienna still lay.

"Hey, my sunshine," Bianca whispered.

She lifted Sienna carefully, drawing her close. The baby's warmth seeped into her chest instantly, grounding her. Sienna smelled like baby lotion, and Bianca breathed in her scent before kissing her forehead. She leaned back against the crib rail, rocking Sienna gently.

After last Christmas, Wise and Bianca became official, and she found out she was pregnant about a month later. When she took the pregnancy test, she was nervous. Bianca had been a single mother with her two children and didn't want to do it alone again the second time around. However, when she saw the look in Wise's eyes when she told him, she knew they would be alright.

When they went to the doctors and found out they were having twins, Bianca became nervous again. But Wise was there once again, letting her know that everything was going to be okay, and it was. Wise was a great father and partner, and Bianca couldn't have asked for a better man to share children with. He hadn't left Bianca's side since she'd found out she was pregnant, and she'd never felt so safe. Together, they had created two beautiful daughters, and they were perfect.

Bianca placed Sienna back into her crib and walked out of the nursery, easing the door closed behind her. She made her way down the stairs and into the living room. Journey sat, curled up on one end of the couch, wrapped in a blanket. A Christmas movie Bianca didn't recognize was playing on the TV.

"Merry Christmas, Mama," Journey greeted, glancing up with a small smile.

"Merry Christmas, baby," Bianca replied, smiling back. "You been up long?"

"Not really, probably about thirty minutes. I was in there with the babies for a minute then came down here to watch TV."

Bianca nodded. "He's so good with them."

Journey smiled knowingly. "Yeah. He really is."

"I'm glad there's no snow this year, and the entire family can be together. I can't lie. I'm excited. And it's the twins' first Christmas."

She glanced once more at the tree and all the wrapped gifts underneath it. She smiled before turning toward the kitchen.

"I'm gonna start breakfast. You want pancakes or waffles?"

Journey didn't hesitate with her response. "Pancakes."

Bianca laughed. "Of course you do. I'm gonna make cinnamon rolls too."

She stepped into the kitchen. The coffee pot was already half empty, and she poured herself a cup before pouring in vanilla creamer. Bianca reached for a mixing bowl, rolling up the sleeves of her pajamas. She turned on her playlist, and soulful Christmas music filled the kitchen. She smiled to herself, as she cracked the first egg, adding salt, pepper, and a little milk before setting them off to the side and mixing the pancake batter.

Bianca was halfway through flipping the pancakes when her son came down into the kitchen.

"Smells good, Mama," Lake spoke from behind her.

She turned, spatula still in hand. "Good morning, son. Did you sleep good?"

"Yeah, I slept like a baby."

Lake stepped fully into the kitchen and wrapped his arms around Bianca, resting his chin on the top of her head softly. "Merry Christmas, Ma."

"Merry Christmas, son," Bianca replied, closing her eyes for just a second. "I'm so happy you're home," she said.

Lake smiled softly. "Me too. Last Christmas was crazy. I went to my friend's house, and the food was awful. I'm glad this year I get to have your cooking. Plus, nothing was gonna have me miss the twins' first Christmas. I would've snowboarded here if need be."

"I know, and I'm so happy. My heart is just as full as the house is."

Just then, Bianca heard footsteps coming down the stairs, and she knew it was Wise. He walked carefully, one twin cradled against his chest and the other nestled securely in his arm. He moved toward the living room and gently placed each twin into their bassinet. Journey's face lit up as soon as she saw them. Sage started to fuss softly, and Journey instantly picked her up into her arms.

When Bianca was finally done cooking, they all gathered around the table. Bianca brought over plates piled with pancakes, bacon, eggs, with a cinnamon roll on the side. Coffee and orange juice sat in the middle of the table, ready to be poured. Wise stood to his feet and blessed the food before sitting back down.

Bianca took her seat last. She looked around the table at her now huge family all eating Christmas breakfast. They were all together, and to Bianca, that was what made it perfect. Bianca folded her hands briefly in her lap, gratitude washing over her so strong it almost brought tears to her eyes. A year ago, she hadn't known this life was possible. She hadn't known her heart still had this much room. However, now here she was, surrounded by even more love than she had before.

Wise caught her eye from across the table and smiled softly, like he understood exactly what she was feeling. She smiled back, knowing that deep down, he did. When they were done eating, everyone helped clean the kitchen. When everything was clean, they all made their way to the living room.

Morning sunlight streamed through the front windows,

bouncing softly off the ornaments on the tree. The lights were still on, twinkling gently, reflecting off gold and red bulbs, handmade ornaments Journey and Lake had made years ago, and a few delicate keepsakes Bianca had collected over the years. Beneath the tree, gifts were stacked neatly, wrapped in red and gold paper.

Journey dropped onto the rug immediately, crossing her legs and looking up at Bianca. "Can we start now?"

Lake laughed, easing himself onto the couch. "You been waiting on this all year, huh?"

Journey shrugged. "It's Christmas, and I know my mama got me all kinds of stuff. It's not my fault that my mama loves me."

Bianca stood there for a moment, just watching them. Wise moved through the living room naturally, handing out gifts and watching as they were opened. Sage and Sienna were in their bassinets, now asleep. Even though they were only two months old, they both had several gifts that were under the tree. Last Christmas, Bianca was introduced to the love of her life. Now, just a year later, they had everything they could have ever dreamed of. She moved to stand near the tree, resting one hand lightly on the arm of the couch.

"I just want to say that I'm really grateful. My entire family is together, happy and healthy, for the holiday, and I really couldn't have asked for anything more." Her voice wavered slightly, but she didn't fight it. "This house has seen a lot of Christmases, but I would have to say this is the best one."

Lake nodded slowly, his expression soft. "Means a lot to us too, Ma."

Wise didn't speak. He just reached for her hand and squeezed it gently, his unspoken words telling Bianca that he felt the same way. They opened every gift under the tree, showing off what they got, while they laughed and conversed. Every time one of the twins' gifts were opened, Journey would take it over to their bassinets and show it to them. Bianca thought it was the cutest thing ever. She loved the way Lake and Journey interacted with their much younger siblings.

By the time they were finished opening gifts, the living room floor was covered in wrapping paper. Opened gift boxes filled with clothes were piled high, along with books, candles, and other gifts they'd all gotten. Lake got up from the couch and grabbed trash bags from the kitchen. He handed one to Journey, and they began stuffing the torn wrapping paper inside. When they were done and the living room was spotless again, they all sat on the couch. Journey grabbed the remote and turned on *How The Grinch Stole Christmas.*

BY THE TIME EVENING SETTLED, the house had changed its mood. The bright energy of the morning had softened. Outside, the snow had started falling, and a light blanket covered the ground. The fireplace crackled in the living room, and soft Christmas music played through the speakers.

The dining room glowed under candlelight. Bianca had transformed it hours earlier. The table was draped in a deep ivory tablecloth with a gold and red runner down the center. She'd placed pillar candles of varying heights along the length of the table, their flames flickering gently. Fresh greenery lined the center, tucked between the candles. At each place setting sat folded cloth napkins tied with thin gold ribbon, a sprig of rosemary tucked neatly beneath each knot.

Bianca stood at the mirror one last time before dinner, smoothing her hands over her dress. She'd chosen a deep wine-colored dress that hugged her softly. The fabric skimmed her curves and fell to her ankles. Her makeup was soft glam, and her hair was in huge flowing curls down her back. Her scent of the night was YSL Libra Intense, and once she put on her earrings and necklace, she was ready. Wise walked into the room, dressed in a cream sweater, a pair of black slacks, and a pair of retro Jordans.

"Wow," he spoke quietly. "You look so beautiful, baby."

Bianca turned to the side and placed her hand on her hip, posing for Wise. "Thank you, baby. You look good too, and you smell even better."

They walked out of their bedroom and headed downstairs. Lake was sitting in the living room wearing a charcoal button-up and matching slacks. The sleeves of his shirt were rolled just below his elbow. The twins were already in their bassinets, dressed in little cream dresses with a gold bow on the front. Moments later, Journey walked into the living room wearing a long, gold dress. With the family all ready, they walked into the dining room to have Christmas dinner.

Once Wise had blessed the food, they began filling their plates with items from the huge spread Bianca had prepared. Conversation flowed easily, as they sat around the table, laughing about past Christmases. Journey reminded Bianca of the year she'd asked Santa for this one particular dollhouse for an entire year, and when she opened the box, it was the wrong one. Bianca laughed, remembering the way her baby girl pouted all through Christmas dinner that year.

When everyone was finished eating, Lake and Journey loaded the dishwasher, while Wise and Bianca put up the leftovers. When the house was clean and all the food was put away, they all made their way into the living room.

"What y'all wanna do? We can watch a movie or play a game?" Lake suggested.

"We can do both. I saw Uno Attack in the hall closet, and I for sure want to play that. I also want to watch *This Christmas* because I haven't watched it this year yet," Journey replied.

"Okay, cool. I'll go get it."

"Hold up. Before you do that, Lake, I would like to say something," Wise revealed.

Bianca looked up, curious. "Go ahead, baby."

He took a breath then another. His hands trembled just slightly. "I didn't plan to do this right now," he said honestly. "Not tonight. I wanted Christmas to be about just that. However, with all the love in this home right now, I feel this is the perfect time.”

The room went quiet. Lake and Journey exchanged a glance, sensing the shift. Bianca’s heart began to beat harder and louder in her ears, not knowing where this was going. Wise stepped closer to her, taking her hand into his.

“Bianca, meeting you changed my life,” he revealed, eyes locked on hers. “I came into your world thinking I was just passing through,” he continued. “But you gave me something I didn’t know I was missing.”

Tears blurred Bianca’s vision, as she realized exactly what was going on.

“You loved me in a way no one else has. You trusted me with your heart and gave me two beautiful daughters.”

He reached into his pocket, and Bianca’s breath caught when she saw the velvet box in his hand. Wise dropped to one knee and opened the box, revealing a beautiful, three carat, princess cut, diamond ring.

“Baby, I love you so much. The best night of my life was the night I met you. And the best day of my life was the day we brought those two little girls into the world. I promise to make the rest of your life just as special as you have made mine. And I hope you would do me the honor of becoming my wife. Bianca, will you marry me?”

Time stopped, and tears cascaded down Bianca’s cheeks. She covered her mouth, as she nodded her head up and down. Finally, she’d gathered herself together enough to speak.

“Yes,” she whispered. “A hundred times yes. I will be your wife for the rest of my life.”

Wise stood and pulled her into his arms, holding her tightly, as the room erupted in soft cheers. Journey rushed forward, hugging them both. Lake followed, clapping Wise on the back.

“Welcome to the family.” Lake smiled.

Bianca held Wise’s face in her hands and kissed him. Just when she thought things couldn’t get any better, here Wise was, showing her that they could. At forty-three years old, not only was she a new mother, but she also now had a wedding to plan. One night at a party had turned around and became the rest of her life.

76

The End! Merry Christmas!

Did You Enjoy?

Did you enjoy the read?
Let us know how much by leaving us a
review on Amazon and Goodreads.

Charge It To The Game 2

Charge It To The Game 3

A Summer To Remember With My Hitta

Snatched Up By A Hitta

Santa Sent Me A Real One For Christmas

Wet Dreams On Lockdown: The Unit Manager

Thug Me The Right Way 2

Thug Me The Right Way 3

Seizing A Gangsta's Heart For The Summer

Yours For The Taking

Wrapped Up In A Hitta's Love For Christmas

By **Nai**

A Set Up For Revenge

A Set Up For Revenge 2

Wet Dreams On Lockdown: The Librarian

By **Ashley Williams**

Trickin' On A Heaux For Christmas

Homie Hoppin' For The Holidays

Wet Dreams On Lockdown: The Female C.O

Letters Of His Love

By **Telia Teanna**

The State's Witness

The State's Witness 2

The State's Witness 3

This Time Won't You Save Me

This Time Won't You Save Me 2

His Summer Side Piece

A Holiday Heist

Healing The Heart Of A Detroit Gangsta

Summer Vows With A Detroit Gangsta

The Promissory

The Promissory 2

A Gangsta's Last Kiss

By **Kyiris Ashley**

Stuck In The Trenches

Stuck In The Trenches 2

By **Huff Tha Great**

Melted The Heart Of A Menace

Wet Dreams On Lockdown: Lieutenant Grace

By **P. Wise**

Merry Trapmas

By **Mia Sky**

Thug Me The Right Way

By **DiamondATL & Nai**

Wet Dreams On Lockdown: The Counselor

By **Paris Iman**

Wet Dreams On Lockdown: The Male C.O

By **Tamyra Griffin**

Wet Dreams On Lockdown: The Captain

By **TN Jones**

Wet Dreams On Lockdown: The Warden

By **Shawnice**

Atlantastan

Atlantastan 2

Atlantastan 3

By **Chris Green**

IN The Streetz

IN The Streetz 2

IN The Streetz 3

IN The Streetz 4

IN The Streetz 5

IN The Streetz 6

By **Tron Hill**

Hittin' Licks For The Holidays: New York

Bandemic

Bandemic 2

By **Freshh Moneyy**

Coming Soon From
URBAN AINT DEAD

Drill
The Hottest Summer Ever 2
THE G-CODE
Tales 4rm Da Dale 2
How To Build Your Credit From Prison
By **Elijah R. Freeman**

Despite The Odds 3
By **Juhnell Morgan**

A Hitman's Gift For Christmas
A Felon's Promise
By **Nai**

Colliding Into Your Love
By Kyiris Ashley

To Die For
By **Tron Hill**

Bandemic 3
By Freshh Moneyy